TEXTS FOR NOTHI?
SHORTER PROSE, _?????1976

Mark Nixon is Lecturer in English at the University of
Reading, where he is also a Director of the Beckett
International Foundation. He has published widely on Samuel
Beckett's work and is an editor of *Samuel Beckett Today/
Aujourd'hui*, a member of the editorial board of the *Journal of
Beckett Studies* and Co-Director of the Beckett Digital
Manuscript Project.

Titles in the Samuel Beckett series

SAMUEL BECKETT

Texts for Nothing and Other Shorter Prose, 1950–1976

Edited by Mark Nixon

faber and faber

Texts for Nothing
Originally published in French in *Nouvelles et textes pour rien* by Les
Éditions du Minuit, Paris, 1954. First published in Great Britain, in the author's translation,
in *No's Knife* by Calder & Boyars, 1967. Published separately in 1974 by Calder & Boyars.

From an Abandoned Work
First published in Great Britain by Faber and Faber, 1958.

Faux Départs first published in the review *Kursbuch*, Berlin, 1965.

All Strange Away first published with etchings by Edward Gorey in 1976 by Gotham Book Mart;
reprinted in 1978 in *Journal of Beckett Studies* and in 1979 by John Calder (Publishers) Ltd.

Imagination Dead Imagine originally published as *Imagination morte imaginez*
by Les Éditions de Minuit, 1965, and in Great Britain by Calder & Boyars, 1965.

Enough originally published as *Assez* by Les Éditions de Minuit, 1966,
and in Great Britain in *No's Knife*, 1967.

The Lost Ones originally published as *Le Dépeupleur* by Les Éditions de Minuit, 1970,
and in Great Britain by Calder & Boyars 1972.

Ping originally published as *Bing* by Les Éditions de Minuit, 1966,
and in Great Britain in *No's Knife*, 1967.

Lessness originally published as *Sans* by Les Éditions de Minuit, 1969,
and in Great Britain by Calder & Boyars, 1970.

Fizzles
Originally published, individually in the review *Minuit* and together as *Pour finir encore et autres foirades*,
by Les Éditions de Minuit, 1976. *Still* first published in Great Britain by Calder & Boyars, 1975;
For to end yet again first published in Great Britain by Calder & Boyars, 1976; five *Fizzles* first
published in English with etchings by Jasper Johns, Petersburg Press, 1976; all texts published collectively, in the author's
translation, as *For to End Yet Again and Other Fizzles* by John Calder Publishers, 1976. *Sounds* and *Still 3* first published in
Essays in Criticism, 1978.

As the Story Was Told originally published in English and German in *Günter Eich zum Gedächtnis* by Suhrkamp Verlag,
Frankfurt am Main, 1973.

The Cliff first published in French as *La Falaise* in *Celui qui ne peut se servir de mots*, Montpellier,
1975; English translation by Edith Fournier first published in *The Complete Short Prose, 1929–1989*
by Grove Press, 1995.

Neither first published in the programme accompanying premiere of text with music set by Morton Feldman, Rome, 1977;
reprinted by the *Journal of Beckett Studies*, 1979 and in *As the Story Was Told: Uncollected and Late Prose* by John Calder
(Publishers) Ltd in 1990.

This edition first published in 2010
by Faber and Faber Ltd
Bloomsbury House
74–77 Great Russell Street
London WC1B 3DA

Typeset by RefineCatch Limited, Bungay, Suffolk
Printed and bound by CPI Group (UK) Ltd, Croydon, CR0 4YY

A CIP record for this book
is available from the British Library

ISBN 978-0-571-24462-1

2 4 6 8 10 9 7 5 3

MIX
Paper from
responsible sources
FSC® C013604

Contents

CONTENTS

Preface

By 1957, Beckett had revolutionised the world of theatre with *Waiting for Godot* and *Endgame* and had also redrawn the boundaries of prose fiction. But the three post-war novels which came to be known as the *Trilogy* – *Molloy, Malone Dies* and *The Unnamable* – brought him to a textual dead end from which he found it difficult to continue. The final words of that last novel, *The Unnamable*, 'I can't go on, I'll go on', encapsulate the tensions underlying Beckett's own subsequent literary movements. As he stated in a letter to Mary Hutchinson, 'there seems to be no "going on", for me, from the *Innommable* [*The Unnamable*]'.[1] In many ways, the prose works that Beckett would write over the next forty years were characterised by his sense that they were 'faux départs' ('false starts'); texts which no sooner begun ended in abandonment, or were discarded after a long struggle to find the path to a satisfactory conclusion. Beckett in these years told a friend that there were two rewarding moments in his creative endeavours, the one where he started a text, and the other where it ended in the waste-paper basket.

The difficulty of writing, and Beckett's own sense of failure, rendered a large part of the corpus from these years ultimately incomplete. Titles such as *From an Abandoned Work* suggest the quality of drafts, elevated to the status of 'finished' works by ever more insistent publishers and public interest.[2] Moreover, the compositional processes of these short prose works are intricately connected and intriguingly self-referential; this is no longer a writer who starts and completes a work, but one who across a wide range of texts realises that there is no possibility of completion. As the surviving manuscripts from this period show, Beckett would start one text, lay it aside to start another, and then return to the original, or amalgamate the two, or abandon both. 'No matter, fail again, fail better', to quote *Worstward Ho*, appears to have been the guiding principle. We are thus perhaps not to view these prose pieces as separate, individual entities, but as an ongoing corpus of writing circling around what *From an Abandoned Work* calls 'all the variants of the one'. Themes, words, sentences and images resurface again and again across this writing, as well as in the works written for television or theatre.

With the exception of *Comment c'est* (1961), Beckett's creative landscape in the years after 1950 is littered with ever shorter, ever more pared-down texts, moving towards what the first *Fizzle* ('He is barehead') calls the 'minima'. One could argue that the Joycean exuberance of the early work of the 1930s and 1940s (aspiring to the master's 'Work in Progress') made way for what Beckett would call his 'work in regress' (note the lower case), the search for a distillation of existential and verbal expression. Moreover, Beckett wrote mostly in French during these years, and then faced the challenge of translating (or rather transmitting) the recalcitrant results into English.

Beckett's failure to find the right way of expressing his failure to express was compounded by the inability of his English language publishers to print his texts with adequate care. As was the case with the journals and newspapers in which many of them first appeared, Beckett's trade publishers in England (John Calder) and America (Grove Press) often failed to meet the challenge of presenting these exacting works. Part of the problem lay precisely in the fact that there were two English language publishers; as Beckett told the English scholar John Fletcher: 'There are often variants between English & American editions because different proofs corrected at different times.'[3] A survey of the different publications reveals that Beckett's short prose has frequently appeared in erroneous forms. This is especially regrettable in the case of these particular works, in which the precision of language – from repetition to punctuation and typographical presentation – is so crucially important.

The present edition takes an eclectic approach to these texts, in so far as all available material evidence – Beckett's manuscripts, typescripts, correspondence with publishers, as well as page and galley proofs – has been taken into account. The most reliable texts thus far of Beckett's post-war prose are contained in S. E. Gontarski's edition of *The Complete Short Prose, 1929–1989*, published by Grove Press in 1995 (hereafter cited as 'Grove 1995'), which has been followed as a base text against which to check the above evidence, being more reliable than Calder's *Collected Shorter Prose, 1945–1980* (hereafter cited as 'Calder 1984'), which is riddled with errors despite the fact that Beckett read proof.

In terms of the ordering of contents, the decision was made to present these prose pieces (as far as possible) by order of composition, while at the same time upholding the 'groupings' seen into print by Beckett.[4] This allows the reader to follow Beckett's developing aesthetic and the dialogue established between texts. The only difficulty with this procedure concerns *Fizzles* (or *Foirades* in French), consisting of eight distinct short prose texts. As John Pilling has argued, Beckett most probably wrote the first five (in French) as early as 1954. He then proceeded to write 'Se Voir' ('Closed place') in 1968, began writing 'Pour finir encore/For to End Yet Again' in French in 1969 and wrote 'Still' in English in 1972. These texts, written across a span of nearly twenty years, were then brought together in French (as *Pour finir encore et autres foirades* by Les Éditions de Minuit) and in English (as *For to End Yet Again and Other Fizzles* by Calder, and as *Fizzles* by Grove Press) in 1976, each edition arranging the texts in a different order. By upholding the integrity of this group, their individual interaction with other pieces written in the interim is slightly obscured. (Thus, for example, 'Se Voir/Closed place', written in 1968, essentially reworks *Le Dépeupleur/The Lost Ones*, which Beckett began in 1966 but then abandoned, and only completed – with an additional final paragraph – in 1970.)

Furthermore, we need to remember that all of the so-called *Fizzles* were published individually in a magazine, before being collected in volume form. The same can be said of many of the works in the present edition. First published as individual slim volumes or in periodicals, they were only later 'collected' in larger gatherings. As his correspondence with publishers makes clear, Beckett acceded to the request for (in John Calder's words) 'acceptably sized volume[s]' by handing over whatever was still unpublished, and allowing texts previously published in limited editions or magazines to be reprinted.[5] This is the background to volumes such as *No's Knife: Collected Shorter Prose, 1945–1966* (Calder & Boyars, 1967) and *Six Residua* (Calder, 1978). At the same time, there is no doubt that Beckett viewed the texts gathered under the title *Fizzles* as belonging together, and the present edition upholds this coherence. I have chosen to place *Fizzles* according to the composition date of the latest text, though the reader should be mindful that they were written across a period of nearly twenty years.

Texts for Nothing

Beckett started writing the thirteen *Texts for Nothing* in French on Christmas Eve 1950, and finished them a year later in late December 1951.[6] He had a clear sense of what he was trying to achieve – as with the three novels of the *Trilogy*, the manuscripts of the *Textes pour rien* show remarkably little revision.[7] However, the English translation proved a rather more arduous affair, and dragged on, or rather off and on, for nearly fifteen years. He began translating immediately after finishing the French versions, in December 1951, but abandoned the task a year later. He resumed working on them in 1958 and again in 1963, but only completed the translations of all thirteen texts in December 1966. They first appeared together in English in *No's Knife: Collected Shorter Prose, 1945–1966* (Calder and Boyars, 1967) – the title is taken from 'Text for Nothing XIII' – and in the same year in *Stories and Texts for Nothing* (Grove Press). Beyond minor issues of spelling, the texts of these stories have remained relatively uncorrupted across subsequent publications, and the current edition makes only two changes.[8] In 'Text for Nothing IX', Grove Press editions give 'resumed by old offence', following Beckett's typescript. The current edition gives 'resumed my old offence', following the French original and Calder. In 'Text for

Nothing IV', 'in the pit of my inexistence' is restored (Calder 1984 gives 'in the pit of my existence' – a reminder that Beckett himself, when reading proof, was capable of missing errors).

The *Texts for Nothing* are often neglected, but in important ways they enabled Beckett to move beyond the *Trilogy* to the works of the later years. If the *Trilogy* still contained a recognisable plot loosely based on the quest narrative, the *Texts for Nothing* foreground a disintegration that the monologue of a troubled consciousness is unable to remedy. As 'Text for Nothing IV' boldly declares, there is 'no need for a story'. Having written these thirteen texts, Beckett again struggled to find a way to proceed. The manuscript notebook containing the second half of the French *Textes pour rien* also contains the drafts of four further prose pieces, all of which were, however, subsequently abandoned. Often mistakenly seen as further 'Texts for Nothing', these pieces differ significantly in terms of nature and tone. They develop a more clearly discernible plot, and they are also longer. Dissatisfied with these drafts, Beckett sought to solve his creative problem by changing language (back to English), a strategy which had served him well after he had started writing in French in 1946. And with his next prose work, *From an Abandoned Work*, Beckett began to concentrate his ideas in ever-shorter forms.

From an Abandoned Work

It is difficult to date the composition with any certainty. Beckett later remembered it as written in 1954/1955, but John Pilling convincingly dates its composition to spring/summer 1954. The first work to be written in English after *Watt* (completed 1945), *From an Abandoned Work* represents a watershed in Beckett's writing. As Pilling has shown, the text as published is far shorter than the original manuscript draft, and thus represents one of the first instances of Beckett's later habit of textual distillation and contraction.[9] Shot through with an atmosphere of narrative incoherence and arbitrariness, the story deals with the memory of three days recounted by a now old man. It was first published (with considerable editorial revision, and with what Beckett called 'varsity punctuation') in the Dublin undergraduate organ, *Trinity News*, on 7 June 1956, and (also with errors) in Grove Press's *Evergreen Review* a year later. The BBC broadcast a cleaned-up version on 14 December 1957 as 'The Meditation', spoken by Patrick Magee, which was subsequently published independently by Faber and Faber in 1958. The text in the present edition differs in one instance from Calder 1984 and Grove 1995 – both of which print: 'Now was this my first experience of this kind, that is the question that immediately assails me' – by restoring 'assails one', in agreement with all the early printings, and as conforming both to the lexical pattern of the text and to Beckett's subsequent French translation; nor is there material evidence that he wanted the change to be made.[10]

After *From an Abandoned Work*, Beckett turned his attention to drama, and, with the exception of five of the *Foirades/Fizzles*, which were consigned to a drawer for nearly twenty years, the only prose work to surface in the next decade was *How It Is*. This longer piece of fiction remains one of Beckett's most remarkable literary and, considering the psychological effort its composition demanded, emotional achievements. Written as *Comment c'est* between December 1958 and summer 1960, and translated into English by the end of January 1962, the novel variously anticipates the poetic starkness of Beckett's later short prose.

Faux Départs

In August 1964, Beckett began a new, longish work in English provisionally entitled 'Fancy Dying'. Ultimately abandoned, it spawned several separate texts of differing degrees of completion. Dating from August or September 1964, and given the overall title *Faux Départs*, four extracts (three in French and one in English) were published in the German literary journal *Kursbuch* (June 1965). These 'false starts' mark a change in Beckett's prose writing, initiating a series, epitomising what Beckett frequently referred to as 'residual' pieces or 'Residua', that concentrates on the workings of the imagination in order to construct geometrically defined 'closed spaces', in which human figures are placed or rather arranged. The opening of the English extract is a version of material found in *All Strange Away*, while the three French extracts anticipate *Imagination morte imaginez*. Taken together, these brief passages represent stages of Beckett's experimentation with a new kind of writing, and their appearance in print showed his increased willingness to allow fragments to be published.

All Strange Away

All Strange Away grew out of 'Fancy Dying' and represents the first in a series in which objects and figures are arranged and rearranged in confined spaces with mathematical precision. It deliberates on the conditions inside this entombed place, paying detailed attention to temperature, lighting and dimensions, as well as to the relationship between silence and sounds, and between degrees of whiteness. The language is minimal, estranged, sparse yet suggestive. An elliptical text, *All Strange Away* responds to the fourth *Faux Départ*, and was abandoned in early 1965. However, in order to raise money for the widow of the actor Jack McGowran, Beckett returned to it, submitting *All Strange Away* in 1973 to the Gotham Book Mart for a limited edition illustrated by Edward Gorey (published in 1976).

In terms of printing errors, *All Strange Away* has fared worst of all Beckett's prose texts. All six subsequent reprints introduce new errors, beginning with the version appearing in the *Journal of Beckett Studies* (1978). Calder's volume publication of *All Strange Away* (1979) introduced further errors. Beckett corrected several of these when he read proof for Calder in 1984, yet inexplicably Calder reverted to the original and erroneous 1979 text in the later collection of shorter prose entitled *As the Story Was Told* (1990). In his notes to Grove 1995, S. E. Gontarski argues that the text printed in *Rockaby and Other Short Pieces* (Grove, 1981) represents the most stable version, since Beckett ostensibly read proof for this volume.[11] However, Grove 1995 at times ignores changes introduced in that volume, reprinting (correctly), for example, 'from ground top of swell' rather than the 1981 'from ground top to swell'.[12] Indeed, the proofs for *Rockaby and Other Short Pieces* are problematic, Beckett having communicated corrections to Grove's publisher, Barney Rosset, by phone.

Imagination Dead Imagine

When Beckett abandoned *All Strange Away* early in 1965, he had already been working (this time in French) on a new text, *Imagination morte imaginez*. Indeed, *Imagination Dead Imagine* was generated from the textual ruins of *All Strange Away*, and Beckett referred to it as the 'residual precipitate' of the earlier text. The two works share many similar features, not least the opening words 'Imagination dead imagine' (which also opens the fourth *Faux Départ*). The French text was finished on 19 March 1965 and published later that year in *Les Lettres nouvelles*, while the English translation was first published in the *Sunday Times* of 7 November 1965. The first independent volume publications were by Calder in 1965 and then in Grove's *Evergreen Review* of February 1966.[13] The current edition retains the text of Calder 1984 and Grove 1995, but deviates in one instance, restoring the comma in 'alone are stable, as is stressed', following Beckett's typescript and the *Sunday Times* text.

Beckett would make the closed space of *Imagination Dead Imagine* the focus of his creative endeavours over the following years, in both prose and drama (and television, if one thinks of *Ghost Trio*). In these works, immobile figures are 'imagined' and positioned by a dying imagination. The detached narration, the mathematical, even scientific tone of observation, connect an abstract and impersonal realm with a residual humanity.

Enough

In 1968, Beckett told Ruby Cohn that he wrote the prose text *Enough* 'aberrantly', between *Imagination Dead Imagine* and *Bing*.[14] Announcing a stark break in its opening line, 'All that goes before forget', it does indeed differ from the two surrounding works, while clearly revisiting familiar territory. In terms of both its unexceptional language and its first-person narrative, *Enough* is more accessible than the other prose pieces from the 1960s and 1970s, and returns to the journey theme that had marked Beckett's work from the 1950s. Written in French as *Assez* between September and December 1965 (and published the following year by Les Éditions de Minuit), the English translation first appeared in the April 1967 issue of *Books and Bookmen*.

The Lost Ones

Beckett started a new work, eventually called *Le Dépeupleur*, in October 1965, but after a struggle abandoned it in May 1966. *Le Dépeupleur* would, in turn, generate a host of other texts. However, in a letter dated 21 March 1970, Beckett told Calder that he was now considering publishing the unfinished work in its entirety. *Le Dépeupleur* duly appeared from Les Éditions de Minuit in 1970, and Beckett added a concluding paragraph shortly before correcting proofs in May 1970. He translated it into English between September and November 1971, and *The Lost Ones* was published by Calder and then Grove Press in 1972 (the latter photoset from the former).[15] The narrative describes a cylinder containing roughly 200 'little people', all seeking their lost ones, or seeking an exit. The scrutiny of the space itself, as well as the rules and behaviour governing its inhabitants, is scientific in procedure and impersonal in tone, and further explores the closed spaces of *All Strange Away* and *Imagination Dead Imagine*.

Ping

The compositional history of the French text *Bing* (translated as *Ping*) is complex. There are ten surviving versions (held in manuscript notebooks and typescripts at Washington University, St Louis), which reveal just how much Beckett struggled to make progress with this text. Indeed, in a note accompanying the manuscripts, Beckett specified that '*Bing* may be regarded as the result or miniaturization of *Le Dépeupleur* abandoned because of its intractable complexities.' Having abandoned this longer text, Beckett salvaged parts in a new composition on 20 June 1966 with the title 'Blanc', which he finished by September 1966 and which was published the following month as *Bing* in a limited edition by Les Éditions de Minuit. The English translation was begun immediately thereafter, and *Ping* was first published in the magazine *Encounter* (February 1967). It was not the only text to come out of the abandoned French piece *Le Dépeupleur*, as Beckett subsequently allowed four extracts (or rather 'rejected texts') to be published in small magazines and art editions.[16]

Although Beckett stated that *Bing* was of the 'same future' as *Imagination Dead Imagine*, he was equally at pains to stress the fact that they are very different. Indeed, the text is closely linked to the failed project from which it arose, *Le Dépeupleur*. His sense of relief at having been able to keep alive at least part of this larger text is evident in his admission, in a letter to Jocelyn Herbert, that *Ping* was 'hardly publishable which matters not at all'. Indeed, one can only suspect that the kind of writing produced by this 'miniaturization' was precisely what Beckett was striving for, 'brief and outrageous all whiteness and silence and finishedness'.[17] Outrageous, yes, in that Beckett fashions a new linguistic minimalism in this text, forgoing verbs, articles, pronouns and prepositions, as well as punctuation other than the full stop, while giving rein to verbal echoes, eye rhymes and repetitions made musical through assonance and alliteration.

Lessness

Beckett was to use the mathematical dimensions of the 'closed space texts' in the compositional process of *Sans*, finished in August 1969 and published that same year by Les Éditions de Minuit. A set of six thematic groups ('families') of ten sentences are arranged in different permutations and combinations.[18]

According to Beckett's foreword to the Calder edition (*Signature Series* 9, 1970), the work deals with the 'collapse of some such refuge as that last attempted in *Ping* and with the ensuing situation of the refugee'. Originally entitled 'Without', the English translation was first published as *Lessness* in the *New Statesman* on 1 May 1970. Sending the text to Calder at the end of March 1970, Beckett ironically referred to it as 'Endless', while drawing his publisher's attention to the importance of being able to see proofs. Beckett made changes to the typographical structure of the text, in proof, first introducing paragraph breaks, before settling for paragraph indentation rather than breaks.

Beckett would continue to write, as he told Kay Boyle, in the same 'scape' as *Lessness*, albeit with dust rather than sand as the organic matter of choice.[19] The result was 'Pour finir encore', which became one of the *Foirades/Fizzles*.

Fizzles

Originally written in French, five of these texts ('He is barehead', 'Horn came always', 'I gave up before birth', 'Old earth' and 'Afar a bird') were published individually in the journal *Minuit* between November 1972 and May 1973, before being collected by Les Éditions de Minuit as part of *Pour finir encore et autre foirades* in 1976. Their composition has often been dated to circa 1960, following Beckett's own note to this effect to Calder.[20] However, there is evidence to suggest that they were written in 1954.[21] It is a sign of Beckett's dissatisfaction that it took nearly twenty years for them to appear in print. Their publication in English was accelerated by the prospect of a limited edition illustrated by the American artist Jasper Johns. Beckett translated them between November 1973 and March 1975, replacing 'Afar a bird' with the more recent 'Closed place' (written 1968). The Jasper Johns edition, published in 1976, undoubtedly galvanised Beckett's trade publishers into requesting their own respective editions of these shorts, so that in that same year *Foirades* was published by Les Éditions de Minuit, and *Fizzles* by both Calder and Grove Press. Together with 'Closed place', Beckett decided to add two further recent prose texts ('Still' and 'For to End Yet Again') to the original five. It is striking that all four editions present the texts in a different order, with Calder following Beckett's own instructions of putting the most recent (and longest) text first, whereas Les Éditions de Minuit roughly followed the order of composition. 'Closed place'- originated in French as 'Se voir' in 1968, and revisits the confined spaces of *The Lost Ones* and *Bing*. Often cited as 'Endroit clos' (the piece's opening words), Beckett translated it as 'Closed place' in February 1974.[22] His difficulties with the composition are evident from the five separate openings of the piece contained in a manuscript notebook entitled 'Fragments Prose début 68'.[23]

Beckett began work on what was to become 'Pour finir encore' in November 1969, and appears to have finished it by October 1973.[24] Beckett allowed an extract comprising a version of the opening seven sentences, aptly entitled 'Abandonné', to be published in a limited edition with illustrations by Geneviève Asse in 1972. He translated the story into English in December 1975, and the text first appeared in *New Writing and Writers* 13 (Calder, 1975) before becoming part of the French and English *Foirades/Fizzles*.[25] The text plays on the familiar Beckettian distinctions of beginning and ending, but the incessant repetition and intractable difficulties produced by the lack of punctuation and unfamiliar syntactical arrangement of words render any summary incomplete.

Beckett wrote the final *Fizzle*, 'Still', in English in the months of June and July 1972 (before finishing 'Pour finir encore'). It was first published in 1974 in a limited edition illustrated by Bill Hayter. It appears, from a letter to Ruby Cohn of September 1972, that Beckett envisaged a series of texts in the same vein as 'Still'. Indeed, he proceeded to write two further related texts, which are given here in an appendix: 'Sounds' (first mentioned in September 1972, and finished in June 1973) and 'Still 3', which was written in June 1973. Both were first published in *Essays in Criticism* (April 1978), with an explanatory essay by

John Pilling, who had convinced Beckett to allow them to be printed. One textual change has been made for the current edition: in 'Still 3', 'lips the ones' has been changed to 'lids the ones'.[26] No further 'Still' texts were written.

It appears that Beckett had as early as 1972 or 1973 begun to think of the first five of these texts as 'Foirades', citing in a letter to John Kobler of March 1973 an entry from his *Petit Robert* dictionary: '*Foirade* – Le fait de foirer. *Foirer* – rater, échouer lamentablement.' As with *From an Abandoned Work*, Beckett's sense of these texts as 'failures' is inscribed in their overall title. Alternately, he at times referred to the fact that 'foirer' related to diarrhoea, and the English title appears to have appealed to him for its connection with the action of breaking wind.[27] It is impossible to tell whether Beckett initially thought of 'Still' and 'For to End Yet Again' as 'Foirades', although the fact that in correspondence with Ruby Cohn he spoke of a 'Still' series suggests that this was not the case. If 'Still' is the odd text out here owing to its being the only piece written in English, 'For to End Yet Again' differs thematically and in terms of length from the other texts. There is a sense that the unity of the *Foirades/Fizzles* editions stems as much from the fact that these eight texts had not yet been collected in print as from any unifying stylistic or thematic coherence, although they share an increasing linguistic experimentation.[28]

As the Story Was Told

Beckett wrote *As the Story Was Told* (in English) quickly, between 4 and 13 August 1973. It was composed for a memorial volume of the German poet and writer Günter Eich, whom Beckett had met several times and who had committed suicide at the age of sixty-six.[29] The story revolves around notions of guilt and punishment as a speaker endeavours to comprehend his part in the interrogation and torture of a man who is being held in a tent nearby. Although the piece is written with ostensible simplicity, it withholds the precise nature of the crime of the first-person narrator, or of the person under scrutiny. It was published in *Günter Eich zum Gedächtnis* (1973), then in Calder 1984.

La Falaise/The Cliff

Beckett's next prose work was also dedicated to a fellow artist. Written in French between 6 January and 26 March 1975 with the working titles 'Pour Bram' or 'À Bram', in homage to Beckett's friend, the painter Bram Van Velde, it was first published as 'La Falaise' in *Celui qui ne peut se servir de mots: à Bram Van Velde* (Fata Morgana, 1975), and remained untranslated by Beckett. The present edition reprints Edith Fournier's translation first published in Grove 1995, and, because not translated by Beckett himself, the French original. Beckett told John Pilling in a postcard dated 7 October 1978 that he was not thinking of any specific painting by Van Velde when writing the text.[30] As with so many of Beckett's later works, *La Falaise/The Cliff* defies generic definition. Although its typographical layout marks this piece as prose, its tightly knit structure suggests a prose poem. Generic uncertainty is more evident still in the final work included in this edition, the very brief text *neither*.

neither

In his responses to the 'queries re prelims to Collected Shorter Prose 1945–80' (sent to Susan Herbert at Calder Publishers and dated 5 February 1984), Beckett stated that 'neither' was not written as a poem and that Calder could include the text in the prose volume should he wish, as long as he appended the note 'Written for the composer Morton Feldman'. Beckett had previously opposed its inclusion in *Collected Poems in English and French* (Calder, 1977). Written in September 1976, *neither* was first published in the programme notes accompanying its performance in Rome on 12 June 1977, set to music by Feldman. The publication history is one of error, mainly of a typographical nature, based on a confusion as to whether to present the text as prose or verse. *neither* was reprinted, with errors, in the *Journal of Beckett Studies* 4 (1979) and gathered in *As the Story Was Told: Uncollected and Late Prose* (Calder, 1990). The work stresses inbetweenness, or rather a 'between-ness' moving 'to and fro' from inner to outer shadow, from self to unself, between poem and prose. The text is here presented without line breaks, according to Beckett's wish that it be regarded as prose.

★

A short preface cannot do justice to the beauty and innovation of Beckett's achievement in the short prose works collected in this volume. The reader will undoubtedly struggle at times with the mathematical, impersonal, uncertain spaces and spare language constructed by Beckett in the years 1950 to 1976. In the 'closed spaces' of Beckett's imaging of consciousness, we are forced to move through stark and harsh landscapes. At the same time, presenting human existence in isolation, these works inscribe the immense poetic force of endurance and of a prose without adornment. In these twenty years of compositional struggle, Beckett paved the way for the luminous works of his final decade of writing – *Company, Ill Seen Ill Said, Worstward Ho, Stirrings Still* and his last text, 'What is the word'. In removing all that is incidental, in textual and existential terms, Beckett can in these pages be seen slowly to write himself ever closer to what he called 'the next next to nothing'.[31]

Excerpts from Samuel Beckett's letters to Mary Hutchinson, John Fletcher, Kay Boyle, John Kobler, A. J. Leventhal, Ruby Cohn © The Estate of Samuel Beckett. Reproduced by kind permission of the Estate of Samuel Beckett c/o Rosica Colin Limited, London.

Unpublished letters from Samuel Beckett to Mary Hutchinson, John Fletcher, Kay Boyle, John Kobler and A. J. Leventhal reproduced with kind permission of the Harry Ransom Humanities Research Center, The University of Texas at Austin.

Unpublished letters from Samuel Beckett to Ruby Cohn reproduced with kind permission of the Beckett International Foundation, The University of Reading.

PREFACE

Notes

1 Letter to Mary Hutchinson, 6 February 1959, Harry Ransom Humanities Research Center, The University of Texas at Austin.

2 In a letter of 3 November 1965, Calder tells Beckett that he is being 'pursued' by readers who believe his publishing house has a 'conspiracy' to withhold Beckett's short prose from publication. Beckett–Calder Correspondence, Beckett International Foundation, University of Reading, UoR MS2073/1.

3 Letter to John Fletcher, 20 May 1972, Harry Ransom Humanities Research Center, The University of Texas at Austin.

4 In establishing the order of composition followed in this volume, I am indebted to Emeritus Professor John Pilling.

5 John Calder, letter to Samuel Beckett, 30 October 1964, Beckett International Foundation, University of Reading, UoR MS2073/1.

6 Several of the *Textes pour rien* were first published in journals before being collectively published as *Nouvelles et Textes pour rien* by Les Éditions de Minuit in November 1955. See the publication list at the end of this volume for details.

7 Note, however, that XIII 'Text for Nothing was written prior to XII', but their order reversed by Beckett when published.

8 To give one example: there is a discrepancy in the hyphenation, or lack thereof, of 'third class' in 'Text for Nothing VII' across all editions, and Beckett himself appears to have been unsure about this. He thus in the typescript adds a hyphen to 'third-class waiting-room' but not to 'third class ticket', and then is not consistent in the proofs of subsequent editions. The present edition consistently omits the hyphen.

9 For an insightful discussion of the genesis of this text, see Pilling's essay '*From an Abandoned Work*: "all the variants of the one" ', in *Samuel Beckett Today/ Aujourd'hui* 18, ' "All Sturm and no Drang": Beckett and Romanticism – Beckett at Reading 2006', ed. Dirk Van Hulle and Mark Nixon (Amsterdam: Rodopi, 2007), pp. 173–83.

10 I am grateful to John Pilling for his help with this variant. Pilling draws attention to Beckett's change of 'me' to 'one' in the original holograph manuscript of the text in the so-called 'Tara McGowran Notebook' held at Ohio State University.

11 Grove 1995 notably follows the 1981 Grove text at three points:

   – 'arse towards d and knees towards b' rather than 'arse toward d and knees towards b';
   – 'to verge' rather than 'to vertex', in measurements of the rotunda;
   – 'Last look oh not farewell but last for now on right side tripled up' rather than 'Last look oh not farewell but last for now on left side tripled up'.

The first two of these instances appear in the 1981 proofs, and are not manuscript changes indicated by Beckett. Both diverge from all other texts of *All Strange Away*, and since there is no clear evidence that Beckett wanted

these changes, they are not adopted in this edition. Indeed, it would seem
that Beckett clearly intended 'toward' to reflect the singular 'arse' and 'towards'
to pertain to the plural 'knees'. The third change is more problematic, as it is
one of two manuscript changes in the page proofs (although the handwriting
is, as noted, not Beckett's). The present edition retains 'left' in the absence of
a clearer understanding of why the change to 'right' should be made. Finally,
Grove 1995 does not consistently follow the 1981 edition, in that it prints
'when' not 'whence' in the sentence 'All gone now and never been never
stilled never voiced all back whence never sundered unstillable turmoil no
sound'. 'Whence' appears in the first edition (1976), and Beckett clearly corrected 'when' to 'whence' in the galleys of Calder 1984; the current edition
follows suit and prints 'whence'. Rather more mysterious is Beckett's change,
in the proofs of Calder 1984, of 'the sun and here' to 'the sun in here' in the
sentence 'This is not possible, there is one, and here another of exceptional
length, in a hammock in the sun and here the name of some bewitching site
she she lies sleeping.' Here I retain 'the sun and here', as is in keeping with the
syntactical repetition established throughout the text.

12 Gontarski does this despite highlighting this change as a 'crucial emenda-
tion' on Beckett's part in the essay 'A Copy-text for Samuel Beckett's
"All Strange Away"', *Journal of Beckett Studies*, 8 : 1 (Autumn 1998),
pp. 121–6.

13 John Calder initially planned to print *Imagination Dead Imagine* together
with the dramatic piece *Come and Go*, but finally, to Beckett's relief, decided
to publish it on its own. The lengthy correspondence on this matter reveals
once again how publishers of Beckett's work were willing to disregard
thematic or even generic coherence in order to rationalise their output.

14 Letter to Ruby Cohn, 19 November 1968, Beckett International Foundation,
University of Reading.

15 The text here follows the versions printed in Grove 1995 and Calder 1984,
both of which correct the errors of the first US and UK editions. However,
this edition corrects the former publication's misspelling of the word 'unfortunate' and the US spelling of 'metres', and the latter's omission of the word
'the' in 'cut off from the ladders'.

16 The penultimate paragraph was published as 'Dans le cylindre' in *Livres de
France* (January 1967), 'L'Issue' with the third and fourth paragraphs
appeared in May 1968 (Paris: Georges Visat), 'La Notion' (second paragraph) in *L'Ephémère* (Spring 1970) and 'Le Séjour', with the first paragraph,
appeared in 1970 (Paris: Georges Richar).

17 Letter to Jocelyn Herbert, 18 August 1966; quoted in James Knowlson,
Damned to Fame: The Life of Samuel Beckett (London: Bloomsbury, 1996),
p. 481.

18 Beckett prepared a 'key' of *Lessness* for Calder, which is now kept at Yale
University. The six thematic groupings are defined in this key as collapse of

refuge, outer world, body exposed, refuge forgotten, past and future denied, past and future affirmed.

19 Letter to Kay Boyle, 6 September 1970, Harry Ransom Humanities Research Center, The University of Texas at Austin.

20 Beckett–Calder Correspondence, Beckett International Foundation, University of Reading, UoR MS2073/1.

21 'Il est tête nue/He is barehead' was most certainly the first to be written, and can be dated to early 1954 by its position in a manuscript notebook held at Ohio State University, before the one-act version of *Fin de partie*. Indeed, John Pilling surmises that this particular text, and possibly all five of these *Fizzles*, pre-date *From an Abandoned Work* (personal communication).

22 Although Calder's 1976 *For to End Yet Again and Other Fizzles* gives the title as 'Closed place' in the contents list, the title 'Closed space' is given in the text. Beckett's various manuscripts of this text give both titles.

23 The notebook in question is held by the Beckett International Foundation at the University of Reading as UoR MS2928. Beckett began 'Se voir' in March 1968, but then abandoned it again in September 1968.

24 Letter to Barbara Bray, 8 November 1969, Trinity College Dublin; letter to Ruby Cohn, 23 October 1973, Beckett International Foundation, University of Reading.

25 The text presented here follows Grove 1995 rather than Calder 1984 in the spelling of 'coxswain' (instead of 'coxwain').

26 I am grateful to John Pilling for alerting me to the necessity of making this change. The word in question is difficult to read in the original manuscript, held at the Beckett International Foundation in Reading (UoR MS 1396/4/51), but considering the emphasis on notions of perception and sight in this text, it follows that Beckett wrote 'lids' rather than 'lips'.

27 Letter to John Kobler, March 1973, Harry Ransom Humanities Research Center, The University of Texas at Austin. Beckett explained the English title of the 'Fizzles' in a letter to Ruby Cohn dated 20 April 1974 as being 'an old noun very close in sense, literal & figurative, to French. All damp, no squib'.

28 In terms of establishing the text, only 'Afar a bird' necessitates a change from Grove 1995, in that the comma in 'last phantoms, to flee and to pursue' has been reinstated according to both typescript and the Calder editions. However, Calder 1984 erroneously introduces a full stop at the end of the text; as in Grove 1995 (and Beckett's original typescript), it is omitted here.

29 The volume in question is *Günter Eich zum Gedächtnis*, ed. Siegfried Unseld (Frankfurt a. Main: Suhrkamp, 1975), 10–[13].

30 I am very grateful to John Pilling for allowing me to refer to this piece of correspondence.

31 Beckett, letter to A. J. Leventhal, 3 February 1959, Harry Ransom Humanities Research Center, The University of Texas at Austin.

Table of Dates

Where unspecified, translations from French to English or vice versa are by Beckett.

1906

13 April   Samuel Beckett [Samuel Barclay Beckett] born in 'Cooldrinagh', a house in Foxrock, a village south of Dublin, on Good Friday, the second child of William Beckett and May Beckett, née Roe; he is preceded by a brother, Frank Edward, born 26 July 1902.

1911

Enters kindergarten at Ida and Pauline Elsner's private academy in Leopardstown.

1915

Attends larger Earlsfort House School in Dublin.

1920

Follows Frank to Portora Royal, a distinguished Protestant boarding school in Enniskillen, County Fermanagh (soon to become part of Northern Ireland).

1923

October   Enrols at Trinity College Dublin (TCD) to study for an Arts degree.

1926

August   First visit to France, a month-long cycling tour of the Loire Valley.

1927

April–August   Travels through Florence and Venice, visiting museums, galleries and churches.

December   Receives BA in Modern Languages (French and Italian) and graduates first in the First Class.

TABLE OF DATES

Jan.–June — Teaches French and English at Campbell College, Belfast.

September — First trip to Germany to visit seventeen-year-old Peggy Sinclair, a cousin on his father's side, and her family in Kassel.

1 November — Arrives in Paris as an exchange *lecteur* at the École Normale Supérieure. Quickly becomes friends with his predecessor, Thomas McGreevy [after 1943, MacGreevy], who introduces Beckett to James Joyce and other influential anglophone writers and publishers.

December — Spends Christmas in Kassel (as also in 1929, 1930 and 1931).

1929

June — Publishes first critical essay ('Dante . . . Bruno . Vico . . Joyce') and first story ('Assumption') in *transition* magazine.

1930

July — *Whoroscope* (Paris: Hours Press).

October — Returns to TCD to begin a two-year appointment as lecturer in French.

November — Introduced by MacGreevy to the painter and writer Jack B. Yeats in Dublin.

1931

March — *Proust* (London: Chatto & Windus).

September — First Irish publication, the poem 'Alba' in *Dublin Magazine*.

1932

January — Resigns his lectureship via telegram from Kassel and moves to Paris.

Feb.–June — First serious attempt at a novel, the posthumously published *Dream of Fair to Middling Women*.

December — Story 'Dante and the Lobster' appears in *This Quarter* (Paris).

TABLE OF DATES

1950

25 August — Death of May Beckett.

1951

March — *Molloy*, in French (Paris: Les Éditions de Minuit).

November — *Malone meurt* (Paris: Les Éditions de Minuit).

1952

Purchases land at Ussy-sur-Marne, subsequently Beckett's preferred location for writing.

September — *En attendant Godot* (Paris: Les Éditions de Minuit).

1953

5 January — Premiere of *Waiting for Godot* at the Théâtre de Babylone in Montparnasse, directed by Roger Blin.

May — *L'Innommable* (Paris: Les Éditions de Minuit).

August — *Watt*, in English (Paris: Olympia Press).

1954

8 September — *Waiting for Godot* (New York: Grove Press).

13 September — Death of Frank Beckett from lung cancer.

1955

March — *Molloy*, translated into English with Patrick Bowles (New York: Grove; Paris: Olympia).

3 August — First English production of *Waiting for Godot* opens in London at the Arts Theatre.

November — *Nouvelles et Textes pour rien* (Paris: Les Éditions de Minuit).

1956

3 January — American *Waiting for Godot* premiere in Miami.

February — First British publication of *Waiting for Godot* (London: Faber).

October — *Malone Dies* (New York: Grove).

May	Shares Prix International des Editeurs with Jorge Luis Borges.
August	*Poems in English* (London: Calder).
September	*Happy Days* (New York: Grove).

1963

February	*Oh les beaux jours*, translation of *Happy Days* (Paris: Les Éditions de Minuit).
May	Assists with the German production of *Play* (*Spiel*, translated by Elmar and Erika Tophoven) in Ulm.
22 May	Outline of *Film* sent to Grove Press. *Film* would be produced in 1964, starring Buster Keaton, and released at the Venice Film Festival the following year.

1964

March	*Play and Two Short Pieces for Radio* (London: Faber).
April	*How It Is*, translation of *Comment c'est* (London: Calder; New York: Grove).
June	*Comédie*, translation of *Play*, in *Les Lettres nouvelles*.
July–Aug.	First and only trip to the United States, to assist with the production of *Film* in New York.

1965

October	*Imagination morte imaginez* (Paris: Les Éditions de Minuit).
November	*Imagination Dead Imagine* (London: *The Sunday Times*; Calder).

1966

January	*Comédie et Actes divers*, including *Dis Joe* and *Va et vient* (Paris: Les Éditions de Minuit).
February	*Assez* (Paris: Les Éditions de Minuit).
October	*Bing* (Paris: Les Éditions de Minuit).

1967

February	*D'un ouvrage abandonné* (Paris: Les Éditions de Minuit).
	Têtes-mortes (Paris: Les Éditions de Minuit).

16 March	Death of Thomas MacGreevy.
June	*Eh Joe and Other Writings*, including *Act Without Words II* and *Film* (London: Faber).
July	*Come and Go*, English translation of *Va et vient* (London: Calder).
26 September	Directs first solo production, *Endspiel* (translation of *Endgame* by Elmar Tophoven) in Berlin.
November	*No's Knife: Collected Shorter Prose, 1945–1966* (London: Calder).
December	*Stories and Texts for Nothing*, illustrated with six ink line drawings by Avigdor Arikha (New York: Grove).

1968

March	*Poèmes* (Paris: Les Éditions de Minuit).
December	*Watt*, translated into French with Ludovic and Agnès Janvier (Paris: Les Éditions de Minuit).

1969

23 October	Awarded the Nobel Prize for Literature.
	Sans (Paris: Les Éditions de Minuit).

1970

April	*Mercier et Camier* (Paris: Les Éditions de Minuit).
	Premier amour (Paris: Les Éditions de Minuit).
July	*Lessness*, translation of *Sans* (London: Calder).
September	*Le Dépeupleur* (Paris: Les Éditions de Minuit).

1972

January	*The Lost Ones*, translation of *Le Dépeupleur* (London: Calder; New York: Grove).
	The North, part of *The Lost Ones*, illustrated with etchings by Arikha (London: Enitharmon Press).

1973

January	*Not I* (London: Faber).
July	*First Love* (London: Calder).

1974

Mercier and Camier (London: Calder).

1975

Spring — Directs *Waiting for Godot* in Berlin and *Pas moi* (translation of *Not I*) in Paris.

1976

February — *Pour finir encore et autres foirades* (Paris: Les Éditions de Minuit).

20 May — Directs Billie Whitelaw in *Footfalls*, which is performed with *That Time* at London's Royal Court Theatre in honour of Beckett's seventieth birthday.

Autumn — *All Strange Away*, illustrated with etchings by Edward Gorey (New York: Gotham Book Mart).

Foirades/Fizzles, in French and English, illustrated with etchings by Jasper Johns (New York: Petersburg Press).

December — *Footfalls* (London: Faber).

1977

March — *Collected Poems in English and French* (London: Calder; New York: Grove).

1978

May — *Pas*, translation of *Footfalls* (Paris: Les Éditions de Minuit).

August — *Poèmes, suivi de mirlitonnades* (Paris: Les Éditions de Minuit).

1980

January — *Compagnie* (Paris: Les Éditions de Minuit).
Company (London: Calder).

May — Directs *Endgame* in London with Rick Cluchey and the San Quentin Drama Workshop.

1981

March — *Mal vu mal dit* (Paris: Les Éditions de Minuit).

| April | *Rockaby and Other Short Pieces* (New York: Grove). |
| October | *Ill Seen Ill Said*, translation of *Mal vu mal dit* (New York: *New Yorker*; Grove). |

1983

| April | *Worstward Ho* (London: Calder). |
| September | *Disjecta: Miscellaneous Writings and a Dramatic Fragment*, edited by Ruby Cohn, containing critical essays on art and literature as well as the unfinished play *Human Wishes* (London: Calder). |

1984

February	Oversees San Quentin Drama Workshop production of *Waiting for Godot*, directed by Walter Asmus, in London. *Collected Shorter Plays* (London: Faber; New York: Grove).
May	*Collected Poems, 1930–1978* (London: Calder).
July	*Collected Shorter Prose, 1945–1980* (London: Calder).

1989

April	*Stirrings Still*, with illustrations by Louis le Brocquy (New York: Blue Moon Books).
June	*Nohow On: Company, Ill Seen Ill Said, Worstward Ho*, illustrated with etchings by Robert Ryman (New York: Limited Editions Club).
17 July	Death of Suzanne Beckett.
22 December	Death of Samuel Beckett. Burial in Cimetière de Montparnasse.

*

1990

As the Story Was Told: Uncollected and Late Prose (London: Calder; New York: Riverrun Press).

1992

Dream of Fair to Middling Women (Dublin: Black Cat Press).

1995

Eleutheria (Paris: Les Éditions de Minuit).

1996

Eleutheria, translated into English by Barbara Wright (London: Faber).

1998

No Author Better Served: The Correspondence of Samuel Beckett and Alan Schneider, edited by Maurice Harmon (Cambridge, Mass.: Harvard University Press).

2000

Beckett on Film: nineteen films, by different directors, of Beckett's works for the stage (RTÉ, Channel 4 and Irish Film Board; DVD, London: Clarence Pictures).

2006

Samuel Beckett: Works for Radio: The Original Broadcasts: five works spanning the period 1957–1976 (CD, London: British Library Board).

2009

The Letters of Samuel Beckett, Volume 1: 1929–1940, edited by Martha Dow Fehsenfeld and Lois More Overbeck (Cambridge: Cambridge University Press).

Compiled by Cassandra Nelson

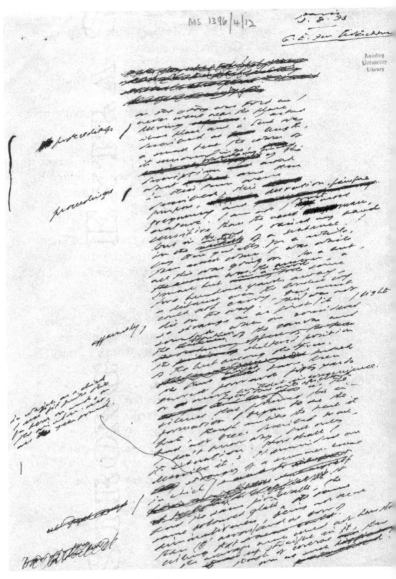

Manuscript of *As the Story Was Told*

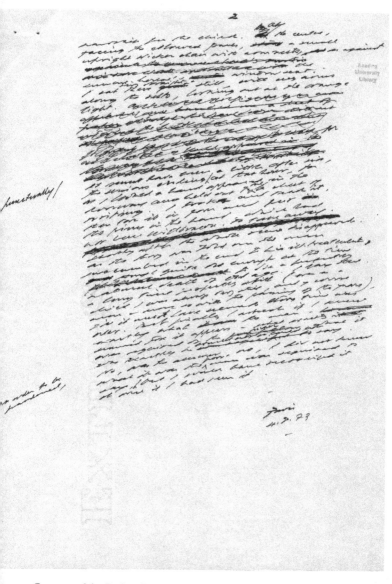

2

functionally /

in order to be
functional /

4.2.73

Texts for Nothing

I

Suddenly, no, at last, long last, I couldn't any more, I couldn't go on. Someone said, You can't stay here. I couldn't stay there and I couldn't go on. I'll describe the place, that's unimportant. The top, very flat, of a mountain, no, a hill, but so wild, so wild, enough. Quag, heath up to the knees, faint sheep-tracks, troughs scooped deep by the rains. It was far down in one of these I was lying, out of the wind. Glorious prospect, but for the mist that blotted out everything, valleys, loughs, plain and sea. How can I go on, I shouldn't have begun, no, I had to begin. Someone said, perhaps the same, What possessed you to come? I could have stayed in my den, snug and dry, I couldn't. My den, I'll describe it, no, I can't. It's simple, I can do nothing any more, that's what you think. I say to the body, Up with you now, and I can feel it struggling, like an old hack foundered in the street, struggling no more, struggling again, till it gives up. I say to the head, Leave it alone, stay quiet, it stops breathing, then pants on worse than ever. I am far from all that wrangle, I shouldn't bother with it, I need nothing, neither to go on nor to stay where I am, it's truly all one to me, I should turn away from it all, away from the body, away from the head, let them work it out between them, let them cease, I can't, it's I would have to cease. Ah yes, we seem to be more than one, all deaf, not even, gathered together for life. Another said, or the same, or the first, they all have the same voice, the same ideas, All you had to do was stay at home. Home. They wanted me to go home. My dwelling-place. But for the mist, with good eyes, with a telescope, I could see it from here. It's not just tiredness, I'm not just tired, in spite of the climb. It's not that I want to stay here either. I had heard tell, I must have heard tell of the view, the distant sea in hammered lead, the so-called golden vale so often sung, the double valleys, the glacial loughs, the city in its haze, it was all on every tongue.

3

Who are these people anyway? Did they follow me up here, go before me, come with me? I am down in the hole the centuries have dug, centuries of filthy weather, flat on my face on the dark earth sodden with the creeping saffron waters it slowly drinks. They are up above, all round me, as in a graveyard. I can't raise my eyes to them, what a pity, I wouldn't see their faces, their legs perhaps, plunged in the heath. Do they see me, what can they see of me? Perhaps there is no one left, perhaps they are all gone, sickened. I listen and it's the same thoughts I hear, I mean the same as ever, strange. To think in the valley the sun is blazing all down the ravelled sky. How long have I been here, what a question, I've often wondered. And often I could answer, An hour, a month, a year, a century, depending on what I meant by here, and me, and being, and there I never went looking for extravagant meanings, there I never much varied, only the here would sometimes seem to vary. Or I said, I can't have been here long, I wouldn't have held out. I hear the curlews, that means close of day, fall of night, for that's the way with curlews, silent all day, then crying when the darkness gathers, that's the way with those wild creatures and so short-lived, compared to me. And that other question I know so well too, What possessed you to come? unanswerable, so that I answered, To change, or, It's not me, or, Chance, or again, To see, or again, years of great sun, Fate, I feel that other coming, let it come, it won't catch me napping. All is noise, unending suck of black sopping peat, surge of giant ferns, heathery gulfs of quiet where the wind drowns, my life and its old jingles. To change, to see, no, there's no more to see, I've seen it all, till my eyes are blear, nor to get away from harm, the harm is done, one day the harm was done, the day my feet dragged me out that must go their ways, that I let go their ways and drag me here, that's what possessed me to come. And what I'm doing, all-important, breathing in and out and saying, with words like smoke, I can't go, I can't stay, let's see what happens next. And in the way of sensation? My God I can't complain, it's himself all right, only muffled, like buried in snow, less the warmth, less the drowse, I can follow them well, all the voices,

4

all the parts, fairly well, the cold is eating me, the wet too, at least I presume so, I'm far. My rheumatism in any case is no more than a memory, it hurts me no more than my mother's did, when it hurt her. Eye ravening patient in the haggard vulture face, perhaps it's carrion time. I'm up there and I'm down here, under my gaze, foundered, eyes closed, ear cupped against the sucking peat, we're of one mind, all of one mind, always were, deep down, we're fond of one another, we're sorry for one another, but there it is, there's nothing we can do for one another. One thing at least is certain, in an hour it will be too late, in half-an-hour it will be night, and yet it's not, not certain, what is not certain, absolutely certain, that night prevents what day permits, for those who know how to go about it, who have the will to go about it, and the strength, the strength to try again. Yes, it will be night, the mist will clear, I know my mist, for all my distraction, the wind freshen and the whole night sky open over the mountain, with its lights, including the Bears, to guide me once again on my way, let's wait for night. All mingles, times and tenses, at first I only had been here, now I'm here still, soon I won't be here yet, toiling up the slope, or in the bracken by the wood, it's larch, I don't try to understand, I'll never try to understand any more, that's what you think, for the moment I'm here, always have been, always shall be, I won't be afraid of the big words any more, they are not big. I don't remember coming, I can't go, all my little company, my eyes are closed and I feel the wet humus harsh against my cheek, my hat is gone, it can't be gone far, or the wind has swept it away, I was attached to it. Sometimes it's the sea, other times the mountains, often it was the forest, the city, the plain too, I've flirted with the plain too, I've given myself up for dead all over the place, of hunger, of old age, murdered, drowned, and then for no reason, of tedium, nothing like breathing your last to put new life in you, and then the rooms, natural death, tucked up in bed, smothered in household gods, and always muttering, the same old mutterings, the same old stories, the same old questions and answers, no malice in me, hardly any, stultior stultissimo, never an imprecation, not such a fool, or else it's gone from mind. Yes, to the end, always muttering, to lull me and keep me company, and all ears always, all ears for the old stories, as when my father took me on his knee and read me the one about Joe Breem, or Breen, the son of a light-house keeper, evening after evening, all the long winter through. A tale, it was a tale for children, it all happened on a rock, in the storm, the mother was dead and the gulls came beating against the light, Joe jumped into the sea, that's all I remember, a knife between his teeth, did what was to be done and came back, that's all I remember this evening, it ended happily, it began unhappily and it ended happily, every evening, a comedy, for children. Yes, I was my father and I was my son, I asked myself questions and answered as best I could, I had it told to me evening after evening, the same old story I knew by heart and couldn't believe, or we walked together, hand in hand, silent, sunk in our worlds, each in his worlds, the hands forgotten in each other. That's how I've held out till now. And this evening again it seems to be working, I'm in my arms, I'm holding myself in my arms, without much tenderness, but faithfully, faithfully. Sleep now, as under that ancient lamp, all twined together, tired out with so much talking, so much listening, so much toil and play.

II

Above is the light, the elements, a kind of light, sufficient to see by, the living find their ways, without too much trouble, avoid one another, unite, avoid the obstacles, without too much trouble, seek with their eyes, close their eyes, halting, without halting, among the elements, the living. Unless it has changed, unless it has ceased. The things too must still be there, a little more worn, a little even less, many still standing where they stood in the days of their indifference. Here you are under a different glass, not long habitable either, it's time to leave it. You are there, there it is, where you are will never long be habitable. Go then, no, better stay, for where would you go, now that you know? Back above? There are limits. Back in that kind of light. See the cliffs again, be again between the cliffs and the sea, reeling shrinking with your hands over your ears, headlong, innocent, suspect, noxious. Seek, by the excessive light of night, a demand commensurate with the offer, and go to ground empty-handed at the old crack of day. See Mother Calvet again, creaming off the garbage before the nightmen come. She must still be there. With her dog and her skeletal baby-buggy. What could be more endurable? She wavered through the night, a kind of trident in her hand, muttering and ejaculating, Your highness! Your honour! The dog tottered on its hind-legs begging, hooked its paws over the rim of the can and snouted round with her in the muck. It got in her way, she cursed it for a lousy cur and let it have its way. There's a good memory. Mother Calvet. She knew what she liked, perhaps even what she would have liked. And beauty, strength, intelligence, the latest, daily, action, poetry, all one price for one and all. If only it could be wiped from knowledge. To have suffered under that miserable light, what a blunder. It let nothing show, it would have gone out, nothing terrible, nothing showed, of the true affair, it would have snuffed out.

And now here, what now here, one enormous second, as in Paradise, and the mind slow, slow, nearly stopped. And yet it's changing, something is changing, it must be in the head, slowly in the head the ragdoll rotting, perhaps we're in a head, it's as dark as in a head before the worms get at it, ivory dungeon. The words too, slow, slow, the subject dies before it comes to the verb, words are stopping too. Better off then than when life was babble? That's it, that's it, the bright side. And the absence of others, does that count for so little? Pah others, that's nothing, others never inconvenienced anyone, and there must be a few here too, other others, invisible, mute, what does it matter. It's true you hid from them, hugged their walls, true, you miss that here, you miss the derivatives, here it's pure ache, pah you were saying that above and you a living mustard-plaster. So long as the words keep coming nothing will have changed, there are the old words out again. Utter, there's nothing else, utter, void yourself of them, here as always, nothing else. But they are failing, true, that's the change, they are failing, that's bad, bad. Or it's the dread of coming to the last, of having said all, your all, before the end, no, for that will be the end, the end of all, not certain. To need to groan and not be able, Jesus, better ration yourself, watch out for the genuine deathpangs, some are deceptive, you think you're home, start howling and revive, health-giving howls, better be silent, it's the only method, if you want to end, not a word but smiles, end rent with stifled imprecations, burst with speechlessness, all is possible, what now? Perhaps above it's summer, a summer Sunday, Mr. Joly is in the belfry, he has wound up the clock, now he's ringing the bells. Mr. Joly. He had only one leg and a half. Sunday. It was folly to be abroad. The roads were crawling with them, the same roads so often kind. Here at least none of that, no talk of a creator and nothing very definite in the way of a creation. Dry, it's possible, or wet, or slime, as before matter took ill. Is this stuff air that permits you to suffocate still, almost audibly at times, it's possible, a kind of air. What exactly is going on, exactly, ah old xanthic laugh, no, farewell mirth, good riddance, it was never droll. No, but one

8

more memory, one last memory, it may help, to abort again. Piers pricking his oxen o'er the plain, no, for at the end of the furrow, before turning to the next, he raised his eyes to the sky and said, Bright again too early. And sure enough, soon after, the snow. In other words the night was black, when it fell at last, but no, strange, it wasn't, in spite of the buried sky. The way was long that led back to the den, over the fields, a winding way, it must still be there. When it comes to the top of the cliff it springs, some might think blindly, but no, wilily, like a goat, in hairpin zigzags towards the shore. Never had the sea so thundered from afar, the sea beneath the snow, though superlatives have lost most of their charm. The day had not been fruitful, as was only natural, considering the season, that of the very last leeks. It was none the less the return, to what no matter, the return, unscathed, always a matter for wonder. What happened? Is that the question? An encounter? Bang! No. Level with the farm of the Graves brothers a brief halt, opposite the lamplit window. A glow, red, afar, at night, in winter, that's worth having, that must have been worth having. There, it's done, it ends there, I end there. A far memory, far from the last, it's possible, the legs seem to be still working. A pity hope is dead. No. How one hoped above, on and off. With what diversity.

III

Leave, I was going to say leave all that. What matter who's speaking, someone said what matter who's speaking. There's going to be a departure, I'll be there, I won't miss it, it won't be me, I'll be here, I'll say I'm far from here, it won't be me, I won't say anything, there's going to be a story, someone's going to try and tell a story. Yes, no more denials, all is false, there is no one, it's understood, there is nothing, no more phrases, let us be dupes, dupes of every time and tense, until it's done, all past and done, and the voices cease, it's only voices, only lies. Here, depart from here and go elsewhere, or stay here, but coming and going. Start by stirring, there must be a body, as of old, I don't deny it, no more denials, I'll say I'm a body, stirring back and forth, up and down, as required. With a cluther of limbs and organs, all that is needed to live again, to hold out a little time, I'll call that living, I'll say it's me, I'll get standing, I'll stop thinking, I'll be too busy, getting standing, staying standing, stirring about, holding out, getting to tomorrow, tomorrow week, that will be ample, a week will be ample, a week in spring, that puts the jizz in you. It's enough to will it, I'll will it, will me a body, will me a head, a little strength, a little courage, I'm starting now, a week is soon served, then back here, this inextricable place, far from the days, the far days, it's not going to be easy. And why, come to think, no no, leave it, no more of that, don't listen to it all, don't say it all, it's all old, all one, once and for all. There you are now on your feet, I give you my word, I swear they're yours, I swear it's mine, get to work with your hands, palp your skull, seat of the understanding, without which nix, then the rest, the lower regions, you'll be needing them, and say what you're like, have a guess, what kind of man, there has to be a man, or a woman, feel between your legs, no need of beauty, nor of vigour, a week's a short stretch, no one's going to love you, don't be alarmed. No, not like that, too sudden, I gave myself a start. And to start with stop palpitating, no one's going to kill you, no one's going to love you and no one's going to kill you, perhaps you'll emerge in the high depression of Gobi, you'll feel at home there. I'll wait for you here, no, I'm alone, I alone am, this time it's I must go. I know how I'll do it, I'll be a man, there's nothing else for it, a kind of man, a kind of old tot, I'll have a nanny, I'll be her sweet pet, she'll give me her hand, to cross over, she'll let me loose in the Green, I'll be good, I'll sit quiet as a mouse in a corner and comb my beard, I'll tease it out, to look more bonny, a little more bonny, if only it could be like that. She'll say to me, Come, doty, it's time for bye-bye. I'll have no responsibility, she'll have all the responsibility, her name will be Bibby, I'll call her Bibby, if only it could be like that. Come, ducky, it's time for yum-yum. Who taught me all I know, I alone, in the old wanderyears, I deduced it all from nature, with the help of an all-in-one, I know it's not me, but it's too late now, too late to deny it, the knowledge is there, the bits and scraps, flickering on and off, turn about, winking on the storm, in league to fool me. Leave it and go, it's time to go, to say so anyway, the moment has come, it's not known why. What matter how you describe yourself, here or elsewhere, fixed or mobile, without form or oblong like man, in the dark or the light of the heavens, I don't know, it seems to matter, it's not going to be easy. And if I went back to where all went out and on from there, no, that would lead nowhere, never led anywhere, the memory of it has gone out too, a great flame and then blackness, a great spasm and then no more weight or traversable space. I tried throwing me off a cliff, collapsing in the street in the midst of mortals, that led nowhere, I gave up. Take the road again that cast me up here, then retrace it, or follow it on, wise advice. That's so that I'll never stir again, dribble on here till time is done, murmuring every ten centuries, It's not me, it's not true, it's not me, I'm far. No no, I'll speak now of the future, I'll speak in the future, as when I used to say, in the night, to myself, Tomorrow I'll put on my dark blue tie, with the yellow stars, and put it on, when night was past. Quick quick before I

12

weep. I'll have a crony, my own vintage, my own bog, a fellow warrior, we'll relive our campaigns and compare our scratches. Quick quick. He'll have served in the navy, perhaps under Jellicoe, while I was potting at the invader from behind a barrel of Guinness, with my arquebuse. We have not long, that's the spirit, in the present, not long to live, it's our positively last winter, halleluiah. We wonder what will carry us off in the end. He's gone in the wind, I in the prostate rather. We envy each other, I envy him, he envies me, occasionally. I catheterize myself, unaided, with trembling hand, bent double in the public pisshouse, under cover of my cloak, people take me for a dirty old man. He waits for me to finish, sitting on a bench, coughing up his guts, spitting into a snuffbox which no sooner overflows than he empties it in the canal, out of civic-mindedness. We have well deserved of our motherland, she'll get us into the Incurables before we die. We spend our life, it's ours, trying to bring together in the same instant a ray of sunshine and a free bench, in some oasis of public verdure, we've been seized by a love of nature, in our sere and yellow, it belongs to one and all, in places. In a choking murmur he reads out to me from the paper of the day before, he had far far better been the blind one. The sport of kings is our passion, the dogs too, we have no political opinions, simply limply republican. But we also have a soft spot for the Windsors, the Hanoverians, I forget, the Hohenzollerns is it. Nothing human is foreign to us, once we have digested the racing news. No, alone, I'd be better off alone, it would be quicker. He'd nourish me, he had a friend a pork-butcher, he'd ram the ghost back down my gullet with black pudding. With his consolations, allusions to cancer, recollections of imperishable raptures, he'd prevent discouragement from sapping my foundations. And I, instead of concentrating on my own horizons, which might have enabled me to throw them under a lorry, would let my mind be taken off them by his. I'd say to him, Come on, gunner, leave all that, think no more about it, and it's I would think no more about it, besotted with brotherliness. And the obligations! I have in mind particularly the appointments at ten in the morning, hail rain or shine, in front of Duggan's, thronged already with sporting men fevering to get their bets out of harm's way before the bars open. We were, there we are past and gone again, so much the better, so much the better, most punctual I must say. To see the remains of Vincent arriving in sheets of rain, with the brave involuntary swagger of the old tar, his head swathed in a bloody clout and a glitter in his eye, was for the acute observer an example of what man is capable of, in his pursuit of pleasure. With one hand he sustained his sternum, with the heel of the other his spinal column, as if tempted to break into a hornpipe, no, that's all memories, last shifts older than the flood. See what's happening here, where there's no one, where nothing happens, get something to happen here, someone to be here, then put an end to it, have silence, get into silence, or another sound, a sound of other voices than those of life and death, of lives and deaths everyone's but mine, get into my story in order to get out of it, no, that's all meaningless. Is it possible I'll sprout a head at last, all my very own, in which to brew poisons worthy of me, and legs to kick my heels with, I'd be there at last, I could go at last, it's all I ask, no, I can't ask anything. Just the head and the two legs, or one, in the middle, I'd go hopping. Or just the head, nice and round, nice and smooth, no need of lineaments, I'd go rolling, downhill, almost a pure spirit, no, that wouldn't work, all is uphill from here, the leg is unavoidable, or the equivalent, perhaps a few annular joints, contractile, great ground to be covered with them. To set out from Duggan's door, on a spring morning of rain and shine, not knowing if you'll ever get to evening, what's wrong with that? It would be so easy. To be bedded in that flesh or in another, in that arm held by a friendly hand, and in that hand, without arms, without hands, and without soul in those trembling souls, through the crowd, the hoops, the toy balloons, what's wrong with that? I don't know, I'm here, that's all I know, and that it's still not me, it's of that the best has to be made. There is no flesh anywhere, nor any way to die. Leave all that, to want to leave all that, not knowing what that means, all that, it's soon said, soon done, in vain, nothing has stirred, no one has spoken. Here, nothing will happen here, no one will be here, for many a long day. Departures, stories, they are not for tomorrow. And the voices, wherever they come from, have no life in them.

IV

Where would I go, if I could go, who would I be, if I could be, what would I say, if I had a voice, who says this, saying it's me? Answer simply, someone answer simply. It's the same old stranger as ever, for whom alone accusative I exist, in the pit of my inexistence, of his, of ours, there's a simple answer. It's not with thinking he'll find me, but what is he to do, living and bewildered, yes, living, say what he may. Forget me, know me not, yes, that would be the wisest, none better able than he. Why this sudden affability after such desertion, it's easy to understand, that's what he says, but he doesn't understand. I'm not in his head, nowhere in his old body, and yet I'm there, for him I'm there, with him, hence all the confusion. That should have been enough for him, to have found me absent, but it's not, he wants me there, with a form and a world, like him, in spite of him, me who am everything, like him who is nothing. And when he feels me void of existence it's of his he would have me void, and vice versa, mad, mad, he's mad. The truth is he's looking for me to kill me, to have me dead like him, dead like the living. He knows all that, but it's no help his knowing it, I don't know it, I know nothing. He protests he doesn't reason and does nothing but reason, crooked, as if that could improve matters. He thinks words fail him, he thinks because words fail him he's on his way to my speechlessness, to being speechless with my speechlessness, he would like it to be my fault that words fail him, of course words fail him. He tells his story every five minutes, saying it is not his, there's cleverness for you. He would like it to be my fault that he has no story, of course he has no story, that's no reason for trying to foist one on me. That's how he reasons, wide of the mark, but wide of what mark, answer us that. He has me say things saying it's not me, there's profundity for you, he has me who say nothing say it's not me. All that is truly crass. If at least he would dignify me with the third person, like his other figments, not he, he'll be satisfied with nothing less than me, for his me. When he had me, when he was me, he couldn't get rid of me quick enough, I didn't exist, he couldn't have that, that was no kind of life, of course I didn't exist, any more than he did, of course it was no kind of life, now he has it, his kind of life, let him lose it, if he wants to be in peace, with a bit of luck. His life, what a mine, what a life, he can't have that, you can't fool him, ergo it's not his, it's not him, what a thought, treat him like that, like a vulgar Molloy, a common Malone, those mere mortals, happy mortals, have a heart, land him in that shit, who never stirred, who is none but me, all things considered, and what things, and how considered, he had only to keep out of it. That's how he speaks, this evening, how he has me speak, how he speaks to himself, how I speak, there is only me, this evening, here, on earth, and a voice that makes no sound because it goes towards none, and a head strewn with arms laid down and corpses fighting fresh, and a body, I nearly forgot. This evening, I say this evening, perhaps it's morning. And all these things, what things, all about me, I won't deny them any more, there's no sense in that any more. If it's nature perhaps it's trees and birds, they go together, water and air, so that all may go on, I don't need to know the details, perhaps I'm sitting under a palm. Or it's a room, with furniture, all that's required to make life comfortable, dark, because of the wall outside the window. What am I doing, talking, having my figments talk, it can only be me. Spells of silence too, when I listen, and hear the local sounds, the world sounds, see what an effort I make, to be reasonable. There's my life, why not, it is one, if you like, if you must, I don't say no, this evening. There has to be one, it seems, once there is speech, no need of a story, a story is not compulsory, just a life, that's the mistake I made, one of the mistakes, to have wanted a story for myself, whereas life alone is enough. I'm making progress, it was time, I'll learn to keep my foul mouth shut before I'm done, if nothing foreseen crops up. But he who somehow comes and goes, unaided from place to place, even though nothing happens to him, true, what of him? I stay here, sitting, if I'm sitting, often I feel sitting, sometimes standing, it's one or the other, or lying down, there's another possibility, often I feel lying down, it's one of the three, or kneeling. What counts is to be in the world, the posture is immaterial, so long as one is on earth. To breathe is all that is required, there is no obligation to ramble, or receive company, you may even believe yourself dead on condition you make no bones about it, what more liberal regimen could be imagined, I don't know, I don't imagine. No point under such circumstances in saying I am somewhere else, someone else, such as I am I have all I need to hand, for to do what, I don't know, all I have to do, there I am on my own again at last, what a relief that must be. Yes, there are moments, like this moment, when I seem almost restored to the feasible. Then it goes, all goes, and I'm far again, with a far story again, I wait for me afar for my story to begin, to end, and again this voice cannot be mine. That's where I'd go, if I could go, that's who I'd be, if I could be.

V

I'm the clerk, I'm the scribe, at the hearings of what cause I know not. Why want it to be mine, I don't want it. There it goes again, that's the first question this evening. To be judge and party, witness and advocate, and he, attentive, indifferent, who sits and notes. It's an image, in my helpless head, where all sleeps, all is dead, not yet born, I don't know, or before my eyes, they see the scene, the lids flicker and it's in. An instant and then they close again, to look inside the head, to try and see inside, to look for me there, to look for someone there, in the silence of quite a different justice, in the toils of that obscure assize where to be is to be guilty. That is why nothing appears, all is silent, one is frightened to be born, no, one wishes one were, so as to begin to die. One, meaning me, it's not the same thing, in the dark where I will in vain to see there can't be any willing. I could get up, take a little turn, I long to, but I won't. I know where I'd go, I'd go into the forest, I'd try and reach the forest, unless that's where I am, I don't know where I am, in any case I stay. I see what it is, I seek to be like the one I seek, in my head, that my head seeks, that I bid my head seek, with its probes, within itself. No, don't pretend to seek, don't pretend to think, just be vigilant, the eyes staring behind the lids, the ears straining for a voice not from without, were it only to sound an instant, to tell another lie. I hear, that must be the voice of reason again, that the vigil is in vain, that I'd be better advised to take a little turn, the way you manoeuvre a tin soldier. And no doubt it's the same voice answers that I can't, I who but a moment ago seemed to think I could, unless it's old shuttlecock sentiment chiming in, full stop, got all that. Why did Pozzo leave home, he had a castle and retainers. Insidious question, to remind me I'm in the dock. Sometimes I hear things that seem for a moment judicious, for a moment I'm sorry they are not mine. Then what a relief, what a relief to know I'm mute for ever, if only it didn't distress me. And deaf, it seems to me sometimes that deaf I'd be less distressed, at being mute, listen to that, what a relief not to have that on my conscience. Ah yes, I hear I have a kind of conscience, and on top of that a kind of sensibility, I trust the orator is not forgetting anything, and without ceasing to listen or drive the old quill I'm afflicted by them, I heard, it's noted. This evening the session is calm, there are long silences when all fix their eyes on me, that's to make me fly off my hinges, I feel on the brink of shrieks, it's noted. Out of the corner of my eye I observe the writing hand, all dimmed and blurred by the – by the reverse of farness. Who are all these people, gentlemen of the long robe, according to the image, but according to it alone, there are others, there will be others, other images, other gentlemen. Shall I never see the sky again, never be free again to come and go, in sunshine and in rain, the answer is no, all answer no, it's well I didn't ask anything, that's the kind of extravagance I envy them, till the echoes die away. The sky, I've heard – the sky and earth, I've heard great accounts of them, now that's pure word for word, I invent nothing. I've noted, I must have noted many a story with them as setting, they create the atmosphere. Between them where the hero stands a great gulf is fixed, while all about they flow together more and more, till they meet, so that he finds himself as it were under glass, and yet with no limit to his movements in all directions, let him understand who can, that is no part of my attributions. The sea too, I am conversant with the sea too, it belongs to the same family, I have even gone to the bottom more than once, under various assumed names, don't make me laugh, if only I could laugh, all would vanish, all what, who knows, all, me, it's noted. Yes, I see the scene, I see the hand, it comes creeping out of shadow, the shadow of my head, then scurries back, no connexion with me. Like a little creepy crawly it ventures out an instant, then goes back in again, the things one has to listen to, I say it as I hear it. It's the clerk's hand, is he entitled to the wig, I don't know, formerly perhaps. What do I do when silence falls, with rhetorical intent, or denot-

ing lassitude, perplexity, consternation, I rub to and fro against
my lips, where they meet, the first knuckle of my forefinger, but
it's the head that moves, the hand rests, it's to such details the
liar pins his hopes. That's the way this evening, tomorrow will be
different, perhaps I'll appear before the council, before the justice of him who is all love, unforgiving and justly so, but subject
to strange indulgences, the accused will be my soul, I prefer that,
perhaps someone will ask pity for my soul, I mustn't miss that,
I won't be there, neither will God, it doesn't matter, we'll be
represented. Yes, it can't be much longer now, I haven't been
damned for what seems an eternity, yes, but sufficient unto
the day, this evening I'm the scribe. This evening, it's always
evening, always spoken of as evening, even when it's morning,
it's to make me think night is at hand, bringer of rest. The
first thing would be to believe I'm there, if I could do that I'd lap
up the rest, there'd be none more credulous than me, if I were
there. But I am, it's not possible otherwise, just so, it's not
possible, it doesn't need to be possible. It's tiring, very tiring, in
the same breath to win and lose, with concomitant emotions,
one's heart is not of stone, to record the doom, don the black
cap and collapse in the dock, very tiring, in the long run, I'm
tired of it, I'd be tired of it, if I were me. It's a game, it's getting
to be a game, I'm going to rise and go, if it's not me it will be
someone, a phantom, long live all our phantoms, those of the
dead, those of the living and those of those who are not born. I'll
follow him, with my sealed eyes, he needs no door, needs no
thought, to issue from this imaginary head, mingle with air and
earth and dissolve, little by little, in exile. Now I'm haunted, let
them go, one by one, let the last desert me and leave me empty,
empty and silent. It's they murmur my name, speak to me of me,
speak of a me, let them go and speak of it to others, who will not
believe them either, or who will believe them too. Theirs all these
voices, like a rattling of chains in my head, rattling to me that I
have a head. That's where the court sits this evening, in the
depths of that vaulty night, that's where I'm clerk and scribe, not
understanding what I hear, now knowing what I write. That's

where the council will be tomorrow, prayers will be offered for my soul, as for that of one dead, as for that of an infant dead in its dead mother, that it may not go to Limbo, sweet thing theology. It will be another evening, all happens at evening, but it will be the same night, it too has its evenings, its mornings and its evenings, there's a pretty conception, it's to make me think day is at hand, disperser of phantoms. And now birds, the first birds, what's this new trouble now, don't forget the question-mark. It must be the end of the session, it's been calm, on the whole. Yes, that's sometimes the way, there are suddenly birds and all goes silent, an instant. But the phantoms come back, it's in vain they go abroad, mingle with the dying, they come back and slip into the coffin, no bigger than a matchbox, it's they have taught me all I know, about things above, and all I'm said to know about me, they want to create me, they want to make me, like the bird the birdikin, with larvae she fetches from afar, at the peril – I nearly said at the peril of her life! But sufficient unto the day, those are other minutes. Yes, one begins to be very tired, very tired of one's toil, very tired of one's quill, it falls, it's noted.

VI

How are the intervals filled between these apparitions? Do my keepers snatch a little rest and sleep before setting about me afresh, how would that be? That would be very natural, to enable them to get back their strength. Do they play cards, the odd rubber, bowls, to recruit their spirits, are they entitled to a little recreation? I would say no, if I had a say, no recreation, just a short break, with something cold, even though they should not feel inclined, in the interests of their health. They like their work, I feel it in my bones! No, I mean how filled for me, they don't come into this. Wretched acoustics this evening, the merest scraps, literally. The news, do you remember the news, the latest news, in slow letters of light, above Piccadilly Circus, in the fog? Where were you standing, in the doorway of the little tobacconist's closed for the night on the corner of Glasshouse Street was it, no, you don't remember, and for cause. Sometimes that's how it is, in a way, the eyes take over, and the silence, the sighs, like the sighs of sadness weary with crying, or old, that suddenly feels old and sighs for itself, for the happy days, the long days, when it cried it would never perish, but it's far from common, on the whole. My keepers, why keepers, I'm in no danger of stirring an inch, ah I see, it's to make me think I'm a prisoner, frantic with corporeality, rearing to get out and away. Other times it's male nurses, white from head to foot, even their shoes are white, and then it's another story, but the burden is the same. Other times it's like ghouls, naked and soft as worm, they grovel round me gloating on the corpse, but I have no more success dead than dying. Other times it's great clusters of bones, dangling and knocking with a clatter of castanets, it's clean and gay like coons, I'd join them with a will if it could be here and now, how is it nothing is ever here and now? It's varied, my life is varied, I'll never get anywhere. I know, there is no one here, neither me nor anyone else, but some things are better left unsaid, so I say nothing. Elsewhere perhaps, by all means, elsewhere, what elsewhere can there be to this infinite here? I know, if my head could think I'd find a way out, in my head, like so many others, and out of worse than this, the world would be there again, in my head, with me much as in the beginning. I would know that nothing had changed, that a little resolution is all that is needed to come and go under the changing sky, on the moving earth, as all along the long summer days too short for all the play, it was known as play, if my head could think. The air would be there again, the shadows of the sky drifting over the earth, and that ant, that ant, oh most excellent head that can't think. Leave it, leave it, nothing leads to anything, nothing of all that, my life is varied, you can't have everything, I'll never get anywhere, but when did I? When I laboured, all day long and let me add, before I forget, part of the night, when I thought that with perseverance I'd get at me in the end? Well look at me, a little dust in a little nook, stirred faintly this way and that by breath straying from the lost without. Yes, I'm here for ever, with the spinners and the dead flies, dancing to the tremor of their meshed wings, and it's well pleased I am, well pleased, that it's over and done with, the puffing and panting after me up and down their Tempe of tears. Sometimes a butterfly comes, all warm from the flowers, how weak it is, and quick dead, the wings crosswise, as when resting, in the sun, the scales grey. Blot, words can be blotted and the mad thoughts they invent, the nostalgia for that slime where the Eternal breathed and his son wrote, long after, with divine idiotic finger, at the feet of the adulteress, wipe it out, all you have to do is say you said nothing and so say nothing again. What can have become then of the tissues I was, I can see them no more, feel them no more, flaunting and fluttering all about and inside me, pah they must be still on their old prowl some-where, passing themselves off as me. Did I ever believe in them, did I ever believe I was there, somewhere in that ragbag, that's more the line, of inquiry, perhaps I'm still there, as large as life, merely convinced I'm not. The eyes, yes, if these memories are mine, I must have believed in them an instant, believed it was me I saw there dimly in the depths of their glades. I can see me still, with those of now, sealed this long time, staring with those of then, I must have been twelve, because of the glass, a round shaving-glass, double-faced, faithful and magnifying, staring into one of the others, the true ones, true then, and seeing me there, imagining I saw me there, lurking behind the bluey veils, staring back sightlessly, at the age of twelve, because of the glass, on its pivot, because of my father, if it was my father, in the bathroom, with its view of the sea, the lightships at night, the red harbour light, if these memories concern me, at the age of twelve, or at the age of forty, for the mirror remained, my father went but the mirror remained, in which he had so greatly changed, my mother did her hair in it, with twitching hands, in another house, with no view of the sea, with a view of the mountains, if it was my mother, what a refreshing whiff of life on earth. I was, I was, they say in Purgatory, in Hell too, admirable singulars, admirable assurance. Plunged in ice up to the nostrils, the eyelids caked with frozen tears, to fight all your battles o'er again, what tranquillity, and know there are no more emotions in store, no, I can't have heard aright. How many hours to go, before the next silence, they are not hours, it will not be silence, how many hours still, before the next silence? Ah to know for sure, to know that this thing has no end, this thing, this thing, this farrago of silence and words, of silence that is not silence and barely murmured words. Or to know it's life still, a form of life, ordained to end, as others ended and will end, till life ends, in all its forms. Words, mine was never more than that, than this pell-mell babel of silence and words, my viewless form described as ended, or to come, or still in progress, depending on the words, the moments, long may it last in that singular way. Apparitions, keepers, what childishness, and ghouls, to think I said ghouls, do I as much as know what they are, of course I don't, and how the intervals are filled, as if I didn't know, as if there were two things, some other thing besides this thing, what is it, this unnamable thing that I name and name and never wear out, and I call that

27

words. It's because I haven't hit on the right ones, the killers, haven't yet heaved them up from the heart-burning glut of words, with what words shall I name my unnamable words? And yet I have high hopes, I give you my word, high hopes, that one day I may tell a story, hear a story, yet another, with men, kinds of men as in the days when I played all regardless or nearly, worked and played. But first stop talking and get on with your weeping, with eyes wide open that the precious liquid may spill freely, without burning the lids, or the crystalline humour, I forget, whatever it is it burns. Tears, that could be the tone, if they weren't so easy, the true tone and tenor at last. Besides not a tear, not one, I'd be in greater danger of mirth, if it wasn't so easy. No, grave, I'll be grave, I'll close my ears, close my mouth and be grave. And when they open again it may be to hear a story, tell a story, in the true sense of the words, the word hear, the word tell, the word story, I have high hopes, a little story, with living creatures coming and going on a habitable earth crammed with the dead, a brief story, with night and day coming and going above, if they stretch that far, the words that remain, and I've high hopes, I give you my word.

VII

Did I try everything, ferret in every hold, secretly, silently, patiently, listening? I'm in earnest, as so often, I'd like to be sure I left no stone unturned before reporting me missing and giving up. In every hold, I mean in all those places where there was a chance of my being, where once I used to lurk, waiting for the hour to come when I might venture forth, tried and trusty places, that's all I meant when I said in every hold. Once, I mean in the days when I still could move, and feel myself moving, painfully, barely, but unquestionably changing position on the whole, the trees were witness, the sands, the air of the heights, the cobblestones. This tone is promising, it is more like that of old, of the days and nights when in spite of all I was calm, treading back and forth the futile road, knowing it short and easy seen from Sirius, and deadly calm at the heart of my frenzies. My question, I had a question, ah yes, did I try everything, I can see it still, but it's passing, lighter than air, like a cloud, in moonlight, before the skylight, before the moon, like the moon, before the skylight. No, in its own way, I know it well, the way of an evening shadow you follow with your eyes, thinking of something else, yes, that's it, the mind elsewhere, and the eyes too, if the truth were known, the eyes elsewhere too. Ah if there must be speech at least none from the heart, no, I have only one desire, if I have it still. But another thing, before the ones that matter, I have just time, if I make haste, in the trough of all this time just time. Another thing, I call that another thing, the old thing I keep on not saying till I'm sick and tired, revelling in the flying instants, I call that revelling, now's my chance and I talk of revelling, it won't come back in a hurry if I remember right, but come back it must with its riot of instants. It's not me in any case, I'm not talking of me, I've said it a million times, no point in apologizing again, for talking of me, when there's X, that

29

paradigm of human kind, moving at will, complete with joys and sorrows, perhaps even a wife and brats, forebears most certainly, a carcass in God's image and a contemporary skull, but above all endowed with movement, that's what strikes you above all, with his likeness so easy to take and his so instructive soul, that really, no, to talk of oneself, when there's X, no, what a blessing I'm not talking of myself, enough vile parrot I'll kill you. And what if all this time I had not stirred hand or foot from the third class waiting-room of the South-Eastern Railway Terminus, I never dared wait first on a third class ticket, and were still there waiting to leave, for the south-east, the south rather, east lay the sea, all along the track, wondering where on earth to alight, or my mind absent, elsewhere. The last train went at twenty-three thirty, then they closed the station for the night. What thronging memories, that's to make me think I'm dead, I've said it a million times. But the same return, like the spokes of a turning wheel, always the same, and all alike, like spokes. And yet I wonder, whenever the hour returns when I have to wonder that, if the wheel in my head turns, I wonder, so given am I to thinking with my blood, or if it merely swings, like a balance-wheel in its case, a minute to and fro, seeing the immensity to measure and that heads are only wound up once, so given am I to thinking with my breath. But tut there I am far again from that terminus and its pretty neo-Doric colonnade, and far from that heap of flesh, rind, bones and bristles waiting to depart it knows not where, somewhere south, perhaps asleep, its ticket between finger and thumb for the sake of appearances, or let fall to the ground in the great limpness of sleep, perhaps dreaming it's in heaven, alit in heaven, or better still the dawn, waiting for the dawn and the joy of being able to say, I've the whole day before me, to go wrong, to go right, to calm down, to give up, I've nothing to fear, my ticket is valid for life. Is it there I came to a stop, is that me still waiting there, sitting up stiff and straight on the edge of the seat, knowing the dangers of laisser-aller, hands on thighs, ticket between finger and thumb, in that great room dim with the platform gloom as dispensed by the quarter-glass self-closing door, locked up in those shadows, it's there, it's me. In that case the night is long and singularly silent, for one who seems to remember the city sounds, confusedly, sunk now to a single sound, the impossible confused memory of a single con-fused sound, lasting all night, swelling, dying, but never for an instant broken by a silence the like of this deafening silence. Whence it should follow, but does not, that the third class waiting-room of the South-Eastern Railway Terminus must be struck from the list of places to visit, see above, centuries above, that this lump is no longer me and that search should be made elsewhere, unless it be abandoned, which is my feeling. But not so fast, all cities are not eternal, that of this pensum is perhaps among the dead, and the station in ruins where I sit waiting, erect and rigid, hands on thighs, the tip of the ticket between finger and thumb, for a train that will never come, never go, natureward, or for day to break behind the locked door, through the glass black with the dust of ruin. That is why one must not hasten to conclude, the risk of error is too great. And to search for me elsewhere, where life persists, and me there, whence all life has withdrawn, except mine, if I'm alive, no, it would be a loss of time. And personally, I hear it said, personally I have no more time to lose, and that that will be all for this evening, that night is at hand and the time come for me too to begin.

VIII

Only the words break the silence, all other sounds have ceased.
If I were silent I'd hear nothing. But if I were silent the other
sounds would start again, those to which the words have made
me deaf, or which have really ceased. But I am silent, it sometimes happens, no, never, not one second. I weep too without
interruption. It's an unbroken flow of words and tears. With no
pause for reflection. But I speak softer, every year a little softer.
Perhaps. Slower too, every year a little slower. Perhaps. It is hard
for me to judge. If so the pauses would be longer, between the
words, the sentences, the syllables, the tears, I confuse them,
words and tears, my words are my tears, my eyes my mouth.
And I should hear, at every little pause, if it's the silence I say
when I say that only the words break it. But nothing of the kind,
that's not how it is, it's for ever the same murmur, flowing
unbroken, like a single endless word and therefore meaningless,
for it's the end gives meaning to words. What right have you
then, no, this time I see what I'm up to and put a stop to it, saying, None, none. But get on with the stupid old threne and ask,
ask until you answer, a new question, the most ancient of all, the
question were things always so. Well I'm going to tell myself
something (if I'm able), pregnant I hope with promise for the
future, namely that I begin to have no very clear recollection of
how things were before (I was!), and by before I mean elsewhere, time has turned into space and there will be no more
time, till I get out of here. Yes, my past has thrown me out, its
gates have slammed behind me, or I burrowed my way out
alone, to linger a moment free in a dream of days and nights,
dreaming of me moving, season after season, towards the last,
like the living, till suddenly I was here, all memory gone. Ever
since nothing but fantasies and hope of a story for me somehow,
of having come from somewhere and of being able to go back, or

on, somehow, some day, or without hope. Without what hope, haven't I just said, of seeing me alive, not merely inside an imaginary head, but a pebble sand to be, under a restless sky, restless on its shore, faint stirs day and night, as if to grow less could help, ever less and less and never quite be gone. No truly, no matter what, I say no matter what, hoping to wear out a voice, to wear out a head, or without hope, without reason, no matter what, without reason. But it will end, a desinence will come, or the breath fail better still, I'll be silence, I'll know I'm silence, no, in the silence you can't know, I'll never know anything. But at least get out of here, at least that, no? I don't know. And time begin again, the steps on the earth, the night the fool implores at morning and the morning he begs at evening not to dawn. I don't know, I don't know what all that means, day and night, earth and sky, begging and imploring. And I can desire them? Who says I desire them, the voice, and that I can't desire anything, that looks like a contradiction, it may be for all I know. Me, here, if they could open, those little words, open and swallow me up, perhaps that is what has happened. If so let them open again and let me out, in the tumult of light that sealed my eyes, and of men, to try and be one again. Or if I'm guilty let me be forgiven and graciously authorized to expiate, coming and going in passing time, every day a little purer, a little deader. The mistake I make is to try and think, even the way I do, such as I am I shouldn't be able, even the way I do. But whom can I have offended so grievously, to be punished in this inexplicable way, all is inexplicable, space and time, false and inexplicable, suffering and tears, and even the old convulsive cry, It's not me, it can't be me. But am I in pain, whether it's me or not, frankly now, is there pain? Now is here and here there is no frankness, all I say will be false and to begin with not said by me, here I'm a mere ventriloquist's dummy, I feel nothing, say nothing, he holds me in his arms and moves my lips with a string, with a fish-hook, no, no need of lips, all is dark, there is no one, what's the matter with my head, I must have left it in Ireland, in a saloon, it must be there still, lying on the bar, it's all it deserved.

But that other who is me, blind and deaf and mute, because of whom I'm here, in this black silence, helpless to move or accept this voice as mine, it's as him I must disguise myself till I die, for him in the meantime do my best not to live, in this pseudo-sepulture claiming to be his. Whereas to my certain knowledge I'm dead and kicking above, somewhere in Europe probably, with every plunge and suck of the sky a little more overripe, as yesterday in the pump of the womb. No, to have said so convinces me of the contrary, I never saw the light of day, any more than he, ah if no were content to cut yes's throat and never cut its own. Watch out for the right moment, then not another word, is that the only way to have being and habitat? But I'm here, that much at least is certain, it's in vain I keep on saying it, it remains true. Does it? It's hard for me to judge. Less true and less certain in any case than when I say I'm on earth, come into the world and assured of getting out, that's why I say it, patiently, variously, trying to vary, for you never know, it's perhaps all a question of hitting on the right aggregate. So as to be here no more at last, to have never been here, but all this time above, with a name like a dog to be called up with and distinctive marks to be had up with, the chest expanding and contracting unaided, panting towards the grand apnoea. The right aggregate, but there are four million possible, nay probable, according to Aristotle, who knew everything. But what is this I see, and how, a white stick and an ear-trumpet, where, Place de la République, at pernod time, let me look closer at this, it's perhaps me at last. The trumpet, sailing at ear level, suddenly resembles a steam-whistle, of the kind thanks to which my steamers forge fearfully through the fog. That should fix the period, to the nearest half-century or so. The stick gains ground, tapping with its ferrule the noble bassamento of the United Stores, it must be winter, at least not summer. I can also just discern, with a final effort of will, a bowler hat which seems to my sorrow a sardonic synthesis of all those that never fitted me and, at the other extremity, similarly suspicious, a complete pair of brown boots lacerated and gaping. These insignia, if I may so describe them, advance in concert, as though connected by the traditional human excipient, halt, move on again, confirmed by the vast show windows. The level of the hat, and consequently of the trumpet, hold out some hope for me as a dying dwarf or at least hunchback. The vacancy is tempting, shall I enthrone my infirmities, give them this chance again, my dream infirmities, that they may take flesh and move, deteriorating, round and round this grandiose square which I hope I don't confuse with the Bastille, until they are deemed worthy of the adjacent Père Lachaise or, better still, prematurely relieved trying to cross over, at the hour of night's young thoughts. No, the answer is no. For even as I moved, or when the moment came, affecting beyond all others, to hold out my hand, or hat, without previous song, or any other form of concession to self-respect, at the terrace of a café, or in the mouth of the underground, I would know it was not me, I would know I was here, begging in another dark, another silence, for another alm, that of being or of ceasing, better still, before having been. And the hand old in vain would drop the mite and the old feet shuffle on, towards an even vainer death than no matter whose.

IX

If I said, There's a way out there, there's a way out somewhere, the rest would come. What am I waiting for then, to say it? To believe it? And what does that mean, the rest? Shall I answer, try to answer, or go on as though I had asked nothing? I don't know, I can't know beforehand, nor after, nor during, the future will tell, some future instant, soon, or late, I won't hear, I won't understand, all dies so fast, no sooner born. And the yeses and noes mean nothing in this mouth, no more than sighs it sighs in its toil, or answers to a question not understood, a question unspoken, in the eyes of a mute, an idiot, who doesn't understand, never understood, who stares at himself in a glass, stares before him in the desert, sighing yes, sighing no, on and off. But there is reasoning somewhere, moments of reasoning, that is to say the same things recur, they drive one another out, they draw one another back, no need to know what things. It's mechanical, like the great colds, the great heats, the long days, the long nights, of the moon, such is my conviction, for I have convictions, when their turn comes round, then stop having them, that's how it goes, it must be supposed, at least it must be said, since I have just said it. The way out, this evening it's the turn of the way out, isn't it like a duo, or a trio, yes, there are moments when it's like that, then they pass and it's not like that any more, never was like that, is like nothing, no resemblance with anything, of no interest. What variety and at the same time what monotony, how varied it is and at the same time how, what's the word, how monotonous. What agitation and at the same time what calm, what vicissitudes within what changelessness. Moments of hesitation not so much rare as frequent, if one had to choose, and soon overcome in favour of the old crux, on which at first all depends, then much, then little, then nothing. That's right, wordshit, bury me, avalanche, and let there be no more talk of any creature, nor of a world to leave, nor of a world to reach, in order to have done, with worlds, with creatures, with words, with misery, misery. Which no sooner said, Ah, says I, punctually, if only I could say, There's a way out of there, there's a way out of somewhere, then all would be said, it would be the first step on the long travellable road, destination tomb, to be trod without a word, tramp tramp, little heavy irrevocable steps, down the long tunnels at first, then under the mortal skies, through the days and nights, faster and faster, no, slower and slower, for obvious reasons, and at the same time faster and faster, for other obvious reasons, or the same, obvious in a different way, or in the same way, but at a different moment of time, a moment earlier, a moment later, or at the same moment, there is no such thing, there would be no such thing, I recapitulate, impossible. Would I know where I came from, no, I'd have a mother, I'd have had a mother, and what I came out of, with what pain, no, I'd have forgotten, what is it makes me say that, what is it makes me say this, whatever it is makes me say all, and it's not certain, not certain the way the mother would be certain, the way the tomb would be certain, if there was a way out, if I said there was a way out, make me say it, demons, no, I'll ask for nothing. Yes, I'd have a mother, I'd have a tomb, I wouldn't have come out of here, one doesn't come out of here, here are my tomb and mother, it's all here this evening, I'm dead and getting born, without having ended, helpless to begin, that's my life. How reasonable it is and what am I complaining of? Is it because I'm no longer slinking to and fro before the graveyard, saying, God grant I'm buriable before the curtain drops, is that my grievance, it's possible. I was well inspired to be anxious, wondering on what score, and I asked myself, as I came and went, on what score I could possibly be anxious, and found the answer and answered, saying, It's not me, I haven't yet appeared, I haven't yet been noticed, and saying further, Oh yes it is, it's me all right, and ceasing to be what is more, then quickening my step, so as to arrive before the next onslaught, as though it were on time I trod, and saying further, and so forth. I can scarcely have gone unperceived, all this time, and yet you wouldn't have thought so, that I didn't go unperceived. I don't refer to the spoken salutation, I'd have been the first to be perturbed by that, almost as much as by the bow, kiss or handshake. But the other signs, irrepressible, with which the fellow-creature unwillingly betrays your presence, the shudders and wry faces, nothing of that nature either it would seem, except possibly on the part of certain hearse-horses, in spite of their blinkers and strict funereal training, but perhaps I flatter myself. Truly I can't recall a single face, proof positive that I was not there, no, proof of nothing. But the fact that I was not molested, can I have remained insensible to that? Alas I fear they could have subjected me to the most gratifying brutalities, I won't go so far as to say without my knowledge, but without being encouraged, as a result, to feel myself there rather than elsewhere. And I may well have spent one half of my life in the prisons of their Arcady, purging the delinquencies of the other half, all unaware of any break or lull in my problematic patrolling, unconstrained, before the gates of the graveyard. But what if weary of seeing me relieve myself, of seeing me resume, after each forced vacation, my beat before the gates of the graveyard, what if finally they had plucked up heart and slightly stressed their blows, just enough to confer death, without any mutilation of the corpse, there, at the gates of the graveyard, where that very morning I had reappeared, no sooner set at large, and resumed my old offence, to and fro, with step now slow and now precipitate, like that of the conspirator Catilina plotting the ruin of the fatherland, saying, It's not me, yes, it's me, and further, There's a way out of there, no no, I'm getting mixed, I must be getting mixed, confusing here and there, now and then, just as I confused them then, the here of then, the then of there, with other spaces, other times, dimly discerned, but not more dimly than now, now that I'm here, if I'm here, and no longer there, coming and going before the graveyard, perplexed. Or did I end up by simply sitting down, with my back to the wall, all the long night before me when the dead lie waiting, on the beds where they died, shrouded or

coffined, for the sun to rise? What am I doing now, I'm trying to
see where I am, so as to be able to go elsewhere, should occasion
arise, or else simply to say, You have merely to wait till they come
and fetch you, that's my impression at times. Then it goes and I
see it's not that, but something else, difficult to grasp, and which
I don't grasp, or which I do grasp, it depends, and it comes to
the same, for it's not that either, but something else, some other
thing, or the first back again, or still the same, always the same
thing proposing itself to my perplexity, then disappearing, then
proposing itself again, to my perplexity still unsated, or momentarily dead, of starvation. The graveyard, yes, it's there I'd return,
this evening it's there, borne by my words, if I could get out of
here, that is to say if I could say, There's a way out there, there's
a way out somewhere, to know exactly where would be a mere
matter of time, and patience, and sequency of thought, and
felicity of expression. But the body, to get there with, where's the
body? It's a minor point, a minor point. And I have no doubts,
I'd get there somehow, to the way out, sooner or later, if I could
say, There's a way out there, there's a way out somewhere, the
rest would come, the other words, sooner or later, and the power
to get there, and the way to get there, and pass out, and see the
beauties of the skies, and see the stars again.

X

Give up, but it's all given up, it's nothing new, I'm nothing new. Ah so there was something once, I had something once. It may be thought there was, so long as it's known there was not, never anything, but giving up. But let us suppose there was not, that is to say let us suppose there was, something once, in a head, in a heart, in a hand, before all opened, emptied, shut again and froze. This is most reassuring, after such a fright, and emboldens me to go on, once again. But there is not silence. No, there is utterance, somewhere someone is uttering. Inanities, agreed, but is that enough, is that enough, to make sense? I see what it is, the head has fallen behind, all the rest has gone on, the head and its anus the mouth, or else it has gone on alone, all alone on its old prowls, slobbering its shit and lapping it back off the lips like in the days when it fancied itself. But the heart's not in it any more, nor is the appetite what it was. So home to roost it comes among my other assets, home yet again, and no trickery involved, that old past ever new, ever ended, ever ending, with all its hidden treasures of promise for tomorrow, and of consolation for today. And I'm in good hands again, they hold my head from behind, intriguing detail, as at the hairdresser's, the forefingers close my eyes, the middle fingers my nostrils, the thumbs stop up my ears, but imperfectly, to enable me to hear, but imperfectly, while the four remaining make merry with my jaws and tongue, to enable me to suffocate, but imperfectly, and to utter, for my good, what I must utter, for my future good, well-known ditty, and in particular to observe without delay, speaking of the passing moment, that worse have been known to pass, that it will pass in time, a mere moment of respite which but for this first aid might have proved fatal, and that one day I shall know again that I once was, and roughly who, and how to go on, and speak unaided, nicely, about number one and his pale imitations. And it is possible, just, for I must not be too affirmative at this stage, it would not be in my interest, that other fingers, quite a different gang, other tentacles, that's more like it, other charitable suckers, waste no more time trying to get it right, will take down my declarations, so that at the close of the interminable delirium, should it ever resume, I may not be reproached with having faltered. This is awful, awful, at least there's that to be thankful for. And perhaps beside me, and all around, other souls are being licked into shape, souls swooned away, or sick with over-use, or because no use could be found for them, but still fit for use, or fit only to be cast away, pale imitations of mine. Or has it knelled here at last for our committal to flesh, as the dead are committed to the ground, in the hour of their death at last, and at the place where they die, to keep the expenses down, or for our reassignment, souls of the stillborn, or dead before the body, or still young in the midst of the ruins, or never come to life through incapacity or for some other reason, or the immortal type, there must be a few of them too, whose bodies were always wrong, but patience there's a true one in pickle, among the unborn hordes, the true sepulchral body, for the living have no room for a second. No, no souls, or bodies, or birth, or life, or death, you've got to go on without any of that junk, that's all dead with words, with excess of words, they can say nothing else, they say there is nothing else, that here it's that and nothing else, but they won't say it eternally, they'll find some other nonsense, no matter what, and I'll be able to go on, no, I'll be able to stop, or start, another guzzle of lies but piping hot, it will last my time, it will be my time and place, my voice and silence, a voice of silence, the voice of my silence. It's with such prospects they exhort you to have patience, whereas you are patient, and calm, somehow somewhere calm, what calm here, ah that's an idea, say how calm it is here, and how fine I feel, and how silent I am, I'll start right away, I'll say what calm and silence, which nothing has ever broken, nothing will ever break, which saying I don't break, or saying I'll be saying, yes, I'll say all that tomorrow, yes, tomorrow evening, some other evening, not this evening, this evening it's too late, too late to get things right, I'll go to sleep, so that I may say, hear myself say, a little later, I've slept, he's slept, but he won't have slept, or else he's sleeping now, he'll have done nothing, nothing but go on, doing what, doing what he does, that is to say, I don't know, giving up, that's it, I'll have gone on giving up, having had nothing, not being there.

XI

When I think, no, that won't work, when come those who knew
me, perhaps even know me still, by sight of course, or by smell,
it's as though, it's as if, come on, I don't know, I shouldn't have
begun. If I began again, setting my mind to it, that sometimes
gives good results, it's worth trying, I'll try it, one of these days,
one of these evenings, or this evening, why not this evening,
before I disappear, from up there, from down here, scattered by
the everlasting words. What am I saying, scattered, isn't that just
what I'm not, just what I'm not, I was wandering, my mind was
wandering, just the very thing I'm not. And it's still the same old
road I'm trudging, up yes and down no, towards one yet to be
named, so that he may leave me in peace, be in peace, be no
more, have never been. Name, no, nothing is namable, tell, no,
nothing can be told, what then, I don't know, I shouldn't have
begun. Add him to the repertory, there we have it, and execute
him, as I execute me, one dead bar after another, evening after
evening, and night after night, and all through the days, but it's
always evening, why is that, why is it always evening, I'll say why,
so as to have said it, have it behind me, an instant. It's time that
can't go on at the hour of the serenade, unless it's dawn, no, I'm
not in the open, I'm under the ground, or in my body somewhere, or in another body, and time devours on, but not me,
there we have it, that's why it's always evening, to let me have the
best to look forward to, the long black night to sleep in, there,
I've answered, I've answered something. Or it's in the head, like
a minute time switch, a second time switch, or it's like a patch of
sea, under the passing lighthouse beam, a passing patch of sea
under the passing beam. Vile words to make me believe I'm
here, and that I have a head, and a voice, a head believing this,
then that, then nothing more, neither in itself, nor in anything
else, but a head with a voice belonging to it, or to others, other

heads, as if there were two heads, as if there were one head, or headless, a headless voice, but a voice. But I'm not deceived, for the moment I'm not deceived, for the moment I'm not there, nor anywhere else what is more, neither as head, nor as voice, nor as testicle, or as cunt, those areas, a female pubic hair, it sees great sights, peeping down, well, there it is, can't be helped, that's how it is. And I let them say their say, my words not said by me, me that word, that word they say, but say in vain. We're getting on, getting on, and when come those who knew me, quick quick, it's as though, no, premature. But peekaboo here I come again, just when most needed, like the square root of minus one, having terminated my humanities, this should be worth seeing, the livid face stained with ink and jam, caput mortuum of a studious youth, ears akimbo, eyes back to front, the odd stray hair, foaming at the mouth, and chewing, what is it chewing, a gob, a prayer, a lesson, a little of each, a prayer got by rote in case of emergency before the soul resigns and bub-bling up all arsy-versy in the old mouth bereft of words, in the old head done with listening, there I am old, it doesn't take long, a snotty old nipper, having terminated his humanities, in the two-stander urinal on the corner of the Rue d'Assas was it, with the leak making the same gurgle as sixty years ago, my favourite because of the encouragement like mother hissing to baby on pot, my brow glued to the partition among the graffiti, straining against the prostate, belching up Hail Marys, buttoned as to the fly, I invent nothing, through absent-mindedness, or exhaustion, or insouciance, or on purpose, to promote priming, I know what I mean, or one-armed, better still, no arms, no hands, better by far, as old as the world and no less hideous, amputated on all sides, erect on my trusty stumps, bursting with old piss, old prayers, old lessons, soul, mind and carcass finishing neck and neck, not to mention the gobchucks, too painful to mention, sobs made mucus, hawked up from the heart, now I have a heart, now I'm complete, apart from a few extremities, having terminated their humanities, then their career, and with that not in the least pretentious, making no demands, rent with

46

ejaculations, Jesus, Jesus. Evenings, evenings, what evening they were then, made of what, and when was that, I don't know, made of friendly shadows, friendly skies, of time cloyed, resting from devouring, until its midnight meats, I don't know, any more than then, when I used to say, from within, or from without, from the coming night or from under the ground, Where am I, to mention only space, and in what semblance, and since when, to mention also time, and till when, and who is this clot who doesn't know where to go, who can't stop, who takes himself for me and for whom I take myself, anything at all, the old jangle. Those evenings then, but what is this evening made of, this evening now, that never ends, in whose shadows I'm alone, that's where I am, where I was then, where I've always been, it's from them I spoke to myself, spoke to him, where has he vanished, the one I saw then, is he still in the street, it's probable, it's possible, with no voice speaking to him, I don't speak to him any more, I don't speak to me any more, I have no one left to speak to, and I speak, a voice speaks that can be none but mine, since there is none but me. Yes, I have lost him and he has lost me, lost from view, lost from hearing, that's what I wanted, is it possible, that I wanted that, wanted this, and he, what did he want, he wanted to stop, perhaps he has stopped, I have stopped, but I never stirred, perhaps he is dead, I am dead, but I never lived. But he moved, proof of animation, through those evenings, moving too, evenings with an end, evenings with a night, never saying a word, unable to say a word, not knowing where to go, unable to stop, listening to my cries, hearing a voice crying that it was no kind of life, as if he didn't know, as if the allusion was to his, which was a kind of one, there's the difference, those were the days, I didn't know where I was, nor in what semblance, nor since when, nor till when, whereas now, there's the difference, now I know, it's not true, but I say it just the same, there's the difference, I'm saying it now, I'll say it soon, I'll say it in the end, then end, I'll be free to end, I won't be any more, it won't be worth it any more, it won't be necessary any more, it won't be possible any more, but it's not worth it now, it's not necessary now, it's not possible now, that's how the reasoning runs. No, something better must be found, a better reason, for this to stop, another word, a better idea, to put in the negative, a new no, to cancel all the others, all the old noes that buried me down here, deep in this place which is not one, which is merely a moment for the time being eternal, which is called here, and in this being which is called me and is not one, and in this impossible voice, all the old noes dangling in the dark and swaying like a ladder of smoke, yes, a new no, that none says twice, whose drop will fall and let me down, shadow and babble, to an absence less vain than inexistence. Oh I know it won't happen like that, I know that nothing will happen, that nothing has happened and that I'm still, and particularly since the day I could no longer believe it, what is called flesh and blood somewhere above in their gonorrhoeal light, cursing myself heartily. And that is why, when comes the hour of those who knew me, this time it's going to work, when comes the hour of those who knew me, it's as though I were among them, that is what I had to say, among them watching me approach, then watching me recede, shaking my head and saying, Is it really he, can it possibly be he, then moving on in their company along a road that is not mine and with every step takes me further from that other not mine either, or remaining alone where I am, between two parting dreams, knowing none, known of none, that finally is what I had to say, that is all I can have had to say, this evening.

XII

It's a winter night, where I was, where I'm going, remembered, imagined, no matter, believing in me, believing it's me, no, no need, so long as the others are there, where, in the world of the others, of the long mortal ways, under the sky, with a voice, no, no need, and the power to move, now and then, no need either, so long as the others move, the true others, but on earth, beyond all doubt on earth, for as long as it takes to die again, wake again, long enough for things to change here, for something to change, to make possible a deeper birth, a deeper death, or resurrection in and out of this murmur of memory and dream. A winter night, without moon or stars, but light, he sees his body, all the front, part of the front, what makes them light, this impossible night, this impossible body, it's me in him remembering, remembering the true night, dreaming of the night without morning, and how will he manage tomorrow, to endure tomorrow, the dawning, then the day, the same as he managed yesterday, to endure yesterday. Oh I know, it's not me, not yet, it's a veteran, inured to days and nights, but he forgets, he thinks of me, more than is wise, and it's a far cry to morning, perhaps it has time never to dawn at last. That's what he says, with his voice soon to leave him, perhaps tonight, and he says, How light it is, how shall I manage tomorrow, how did I manage yesterday, pah it's the end, it's a far cry to morning, and who's this speaking in me, and who's this disowning me, as though I had taken his place, usurped his life, that old shame that kept me from living, the shame of my living that kept me from living, and so on, muttering, the old inanities, his chin on his heart, his arms dangling, sagging at the knees, in the night. Will they succeed in slipping me into him, the memory and dream of me, into him still living, aren't I there already, wasn't I always there, like a stain of remorse, is that my night and contumacy, in the dungeons of this moribund, and from now till he dies my last chance to have been, and who is this raving now, pah there are voices everywhere, ears everywhere, one who speaks saying, without ceasing to speak, Who's speaking?, and one who hears, mute, uncomprehending, far from all, and bodies everywhere, bent, fixed, where my prospects must be just as good, just as poor, as in this firstcomer. And none will wait, he no more than the others, none ever waited to die for me to live in him, so as to die with him, but quick quick all die, saying, Quick quick let us die, without him, as we lived, before it's too late, lest we won't have lived. And this other now, obviously, what's to be said of this latest other, with his babble of homeless mes and untenanted hims, this other without number or person whose abandoned being we haunt, nothing. There's a pretty three in one, and what a one, what a no one. So, I'm supposed to say now, it's the moment, so that's the earth, these expiring vitals set aside for me which no sooner taken over would be set aside for another, many thanks, and here the laugh, the long silent guffaw of the knowing non-exister, at hearing ascribed to him such pregnant words, confess you're not the man you were, you'll end up riding a bicycle. That's the accountants' chorus, opining like a single man, and there are more to come, all the peoples of the earth would not suffice, at the end of the billions you'd need a god, unwitnessed witness of witnesses, what a blessing it's all down the drain, nothing ever as much as begun, nothing ever but nothing and never, nothing ever but lifeless words.

XIII

Weaker still the weak old voice that tried in vain to make me, dying away as much as to say it's going from here to try else-where, or dying down, there's no telling, as much as to say it's going to cease, give up trying. No voice ever but it in my life, it says, if speaking of me one can speak of life, and it can, it still can, or if not of life, there it dies, if this, if that, if speaking of me, there it dies, but who can the greater can the less, once you've spoken of me you can speak of anything, up to the point where, up to the time when, there it dies, it can't go on, it's been its death, speaking of me, here or elsewhere, it says, it murmurs. Whose voice, no one's, there is no one, there's a voice without a mouth, and somewhere a kind of hearing, something compelled to hear, and somewhere a hand, it calls that a hand, it wants to make a hand, or if not a hand something somewhere that can leave a trace, of what is made, of what is said, you can't do with less, no, that's romancing, more romancing, there is nothing but a voice murmuring a trace. A trace, it wants to leave a trace, yes, like air leaves among the leaves, among the grass, among the sand, it's with that it would make a life, but soon it will be the end, it won't be long now, there won't be any life, there won't have been any life, there will be silence, the air quite still that trembled once an instant, the tiny flurry of dust quite settled. Air, dust, there is no air here, nor anything to make dust, and to speak of instants, to speak of once, is to speak of nothing, but there it is, those are the expressions it employs. It has always spoken, it will always speak, of things that don't exist, or only exist elsewhere, if you like, if you must, if that may be called existing. Unfortunately it is not a question of elsewhere, but of here, ah there are the words out at last, out again, that was the only chance, get out of here and go elsewhere, go where time passes and atoms assemble an instant, where the voice belongs perhaps, where it sometimes says it must have belonged, to be able to speak of such figments. Yes, out of here, but how when here is empty, not a speck of dust, not a breath, the voice's breath alone, it breathes in vain, nothing is made. If I were here, if it could have made me, how I would pity it, for having spoken so long in vain, no, that won't do, it wouldn't have spoken in vain if I were here, and I wouldn't pity it if it had made me, I'd curse it, or bless it, it would be in my mouth, cursing, blessing, whom, what, it wouldn't be able to say, in my mouth it wouldn't have much to say, that had so much to say in vain. But this pity, all the same, it wonders, this pity that is in the air, though no air here for pity, but it's the expression, it wonders should it stop and wonder what pity is doing here and if it's not hope gleaming, another expression, evilly among the imaginary ashes, the faint hope of a faint being after all, human in kind, tears in its eyes before they've had time to open, no, no more stopping and wondering, about that or anything else, nothing will stop it any more, in its fall, or in its rise, perhaps it will end on a castrato scream. True there was never much talk of the heart, literal or figurative, but that's no reason for hoping, what, that one day there will be one, to send up above to break in the galanty show, pity. But what more is it waiting for now, when there's no doubt left, no choice left, to stick a sock in its death-rattle, yet another locution. To have rounded off its cock-and-bullshit in a coda worthy of the rest? Last everlasting questions, infant languors in the end sheets, last images, end of dream, of being past, passing and to be, end of lie. Is it possible, is that the possible thing at last, the extinction of this black nothing and its impossible shades, the end of the farce of making and the silencing of silence, it wonders, that voice which is silence, or it's me, there's no telling, it's all the same dream, the same silence, it and me, it and him, him and me, and all our train, and all theirs, and all theirs, but whose, whose dream, whose silence, old questions, last questions, ours who are dream and silence, but it's ended, we're ended who never were, soon there will be nothing where there was never anything, last images. And whose the shame, at every mute micromillisyllable, and unslakable infinity of remorse delving deeper ever deeper in its bite, at having to hear, having to say, fainter than the faintest murmur, so many lies, so many times the same lie lyingly denied, whose the screaming silence of no's knife in yes's wound, it wonders. And wonders what has become of the wish to know, it is gone, the heart is gone, the head is gone, no one feels anything, asks anything, seeks anything, says anything, hears anything, there is only silence. It's not true, yes, it's true, it's true and it's not true, there is silence and there is not silence, there is no one and there is someone, nothing prevents anything. And were the voice to cease quite at last, the old ceasing voice, it would not be true, as it is not true that it speaks, it can't speak, it can't cease. And were there one day to be here, where there are no days, which is no place, born of the impossible voice the unmakable being, and a gleam of light, still all would be silent and empty and dark, as now, as soon now, when all will be ended, all said, it says, it murmurs.

From an Abandoned Work

Up bright and early that day, I was young then, feeling awful, and out, mother hanging out of the window in her nightdress weeping and waving. Nice fresh morning, bright too early as so often. Feeling really awful, very violent. The sky would soon darken and rain fall and go on falling, all day, till evening. Then blue and sun again a second, then night. Feeling all this, how violent and the kind of day, I stopped and turned. So back with bowed head on the look out for a snail, slug or worm. Great love in my heart too for all things still and rooted, bushes, boulders and the like, too numerous to mention, even the flowers of the field, not for the world when in my right senses would I ever touch one, to pluck it. Whereas a bird now, or a butterfly, fluttering about and getting in my way, all moving things, getting in my path, a slug now, getting under my feet, no, no mercy. Not that I'd go out of my way to get at them, no, at a distance often they seemed still, then a moment later they were upon me. Birds with my piercing sight I have seen flying so high, so far, that they seemed at rest, then the next minute they were all about me, crows have done this. Ducks are perhaps the worst, to be suddenly stamping and stumbling in the midst of ducks, or hens, any class of poultry, few things are worse. Nor will I go out of my way to avoid such things, when avoidable, no, I simply will not go out of my way, though I have never in my life been on my way anywhere, but simply on my way. And in this way I have gone through great thickets, bleeding, and deep into bogs, water too, even the sea in some moods and been carried out of my course, or driven back, so as not to drown. And that is perhaps how I shall die at last if they don't catch me, I mean drowned, or in fire, yes, perhaps that is how I shall do it at last, walking furious headlong into fire and dying burnt to bits. Then I raised my eyes and saw my mother still in the window waving, waving me back

57

or on I don't know, or just waving, in sad helpless love, and I heard faintly her cries. The window-frame was green, pale, the house-wall grey and my mother white and so thin I could see past her (piercing sight I had then) into the dark of the room, and on all that full the not long risen sun, and all small because of the distance, very pretty really the whole thing, I remember it, the old grey and then the thin green surround and the thin white against the dark, if only she could have been still and let me look at it all. No, for once I wanted to stand and look at something I couldn't with her there waving and fluttering and swaying in and out of the window as though she were doing exercises, and for all I know she may have been, not bothering about me at all. No tenacity of purpose, that was another thing I didn't like in her. One week it would be exercises, and the next prayers and Bible reading, and the next gardening, and the next playing the piano and singing, that was awful, and then just lying about and resting, always changing. Not that it mattered to me, I was always out. But let me get on now with the day I have hit on to begin with, any other would have done as well, yes, on with it and out of my way and on to another, enough of my mother for the moment. Well then for a time all well, no trouble, no birds at me, nothing across my path except at a great distance a white horse followed by a boy, or it might have been a small man or woman. This is the only completely white horse I remember, what I believe the Germans call a Schimmel, oh I was very quick as a boy and picked up a lot of hard knowledge, Schimmel, nice word, for an English speaker. The sun was full upon it, as shortly before on my mother, and it seemed to have a red band or stripe running down its side, I thought perhaps a bellyband, perhaps the horse was going somewhere to be harnessed, to a trap or suchlike. It crossed my path a long way off, then vanished behind greenery, I suppose, all I noticed was the sudden appearance of the horse, then disappearance. It was bright white, with the sun on it, I had never seen such a horse, though often heard of them, and never saw another. White I must say has always affected me strongly, all white things, sheets, walls and so on, even flowers, and then just white, the thought of white, without more. But let me get on with this day and get it over. All well then for a time, just the violence and then this white horse, when suddenly I flew into a most savage rage, really blinding. Now why this sudden rage I really don't know, these sudden rages, they made my life a misery. Many other things too did this, my sore throat for example, I have never known what it is to be without a sore throat, but the rages were the worst, like a great wind suddenly rising in me, no, I can't describe. It wasn't the violence getting worse in any case, nothing to do with that, some days I would be feeling violent all day and never have a rage, other days quite quiet for me and have four or five. No, there's no accounting for it, there's no accounting for anything, with a mind like the one I always had, always on the alert against itself, I'll come back on this perhaps when I feel less weak. There was a time I tried to get relief by beating my head against something, but I gave it up. The best thing I found was to start running. Perhaps I should mention here I was a very slow walker. I didn't really dally or loiter in any way, just walked very slowly, little short steps and the feet very slow through the air. On the other hand I must have been quite one of the fastest runners the world has ever seen, over a short distance, five or ten yards, in a second I was there. But I could not go on at that speed, not for breathlessness, it was mental, all is mental, figments. Now the jog trot on the other hand, I could no more do that than I could fly. No, with me all was slow, and then these flashes, or gushes, vent the pent, that was one of those things I used to say, over and over, as I went along, vent the pent, vent the pent. Fortunately my father died when I was a boy, otherwise I might have been a professor, he had set his heart on it. A very fair scholar I was too, no thought, but a great memory. One day I told him about Milton's cosmology, away up in the mountains we were, resting against a huge rock looking out to sea, that impressed him greatly. Love too, often in my thoughts, when a boy, but not a great deal compared to other boys, it kept me awake I found. Never loved anyone I think, I'd remember. Except in my dreams, and there it was animals, dream animals, nothing like what you see walking about the country, I couldn't describe them, lovely creatures they were, white mostly. In a way perhaps it's a pity, a good woman might have been the making of me, I might be sprawling in the sun now sucking my pipe and patting the bottoms of the third and fourth generation, looked up to and respected, wondering what there was for dinner, instead of stravaging the same old roads in all weathers, I was never much of a one for new ground. No, I regret nothing, all I regret is having been born, dying is such a long tiresome business I always found. But let me get on now from where I left off, the white horse and then the rage, no connexion I suppose. But why go on with all this, I don't know, some day I must end, why not now. But these are thoughts, not mine, no matter, shame upon me. Now I am old and weak, in pain and weakness murmur why and pause, and the old thoughts well up in me and over into my voice, the old thoughts born with me and grown with me and kept under, there's another. No, back to that far day, any far day, and from the dim granted ground to its things and sky the eyes raised and back again, raised again and back again again, and the feet going nowhere only somehow home, in the morning out from home and in the evening back home again, and the sound of my voice all day long muttering the same old things I don't listen to, not even mine it was at the end of the day, like a marmoset sitting on my shoulder with its bushy tail, keeping me company. All this talking, very low and hoarse, no wonder I had a sore throat. Perhaps I should mention here that I never talked to anyone, I think my father was the last one I talked to. My mother was the same, never talked, never answered, since my father died. I asked her for the money, I can't go back on that now, those must have been my last words to her. Sometimes she cried out on me, or implored, but never long, just a few cries, then if I looked up the poor old thin lips pressed tight together and the body turned away and just the corners of the eyes on me, but it was rare. Sometimes in the night I heard her, talking to herself I suppose, or praying out loud, or reading out loud, or reciting her hymns, poor woman. Well after the horse and the rage I don't know, just on, then I suppose the slow turn, wheeling more and more to the one or other hand, till facing home, then home. Ah my father and mother, to think they are probably in paradise, they were so good. Let me go to hell, that's all I ask, and go on cursing them there, and them look down and hear me, that might take some shine off their bliss. Yes, I believe all their blather about the life to come, it cheers me up, and unhappiness like mine, there's no annihilating that. I was mad of course and still am, but harmless, I passed for harmless, that's a good one. Not of course that I was really mad, just strange, a little strange, and with every passing year a little stranger, there can be few stranger creatures going about than me at the present day. My father, did I kill him too as well as my mother, perhaps in a way I did, but I can't go into that now, much too old and weak. The questions float up as I go along and leave me very confused, breaking up I am. Suddenly they are there, no, they float up, out of an old depth, and hover and linger before they die away, questions that when I was in my right mind would not have survived one second, no, but atomized they would have been, before as much as formed, atomized. In twos often they came, one hard on the other, thus, How shall I go on another day? and then, How did I ever go on another day? Or, Did I kill my father? and then, Did I ever kill anyone? That kind of way, to the general from the particular I suppose you might say, question and answer too in a way, very addling. I strive with them as best I can, quickening my step when they come on, tossing my head from side to side and up and down, staring agonizedly at this and that, increasing my murmur to a scream, these are helps. But they should not be necessary, something is wrong here, if it was the end I would not so much mind, but how often I have said, in my life, before some new awful thing, It is the end, and it was not the end, and yet the end cannot be far off now, I shall fall as I go along and stay down or curl up for the night as usual among the rocks and before morning be gone. Oh I know I too shall cease and be as when I was not yet, only all over instead of in store, that makes me happy, often now my murmur falters and dies and I weep for happiness as I go along and for love of this old earth that has carried me so long and whose uncomplainingness will soon be mine. Just under the surface I shall be, all together at first, then separate and drift, through all the earth and perhaps in the end through a cliff into the sea, something of me. A ton of worms in an acre, that is a wonderful thought, a ton of worms, I believe it. Where did I get it, from a dream, or a book read in a nook when a boy, or a word overheard as I went along, or in me all along and kept under till it could give me joy, these are the kind of horrid thoughts I have to contend with in the way I have said. Now is there nothing to add to this day with the white horse and white mother in the window, please read again my descriptions of these, before I get on to some other day at a later time, nothing to add before I move on in time skipping hundreds and even thousands of days in a way I could not at the time, but had to get through some-how until I came to the one I am coming to now, no, nothing, all has gone but mother in the window, the violence, rage and rain. So on to this second day and get it over and out of the way and on to the next. What happens now is I was set on and pursued by a family or tribe, I do not know, of stoats, a most extraordi-nary thing, I think they were stoats. Indeed if I may say so I think I was fortunate to get off with my life, strange expression, it does not sound right somehow. Anyone else would have been bitten and bled to death, perhaps sucked white, like a rabbit, there is that word white again. I know I could never think, but if I could have, and then had, I would just have lain down and let myself be destroyed, as the rabbit does. But let me start as always with the morning and the getting out. When a day comes back, what-ever the reason, then its morning and its evening too are there, though in themselves quite unremarkable, the going out and coming home, there is a remarkable thing I find. So up then in the grey of dawn, very weak and shaky after an atrocious night little dreaming what lay in store, out and off. What time of year, I really do not know, does it matter. Not wet really, but dripping, everything dripping, the day might rise, did it, no, drip drip all day long, no sun, no change of light, dim all day, and still, not a breath, till night, then black, and a little wind, I saw some stars, as I neared home. My stick of course, by a merciful providence, I shall not say this again, when not mentioned my stick is in my hand, as I go along. But not my long coat, just my jacket, I could never bear the long coat, flapping about my legs, or rather one day suddenly I turned against it, a sudden violent dislike. Often when dressed to go I would take it out and put it on, then stand in the middle of the room unable to move, until at last I could take it off and put it back on its hanger, in the cupboard. But I was hardly down the stairs and out into the air when the stick fell from my hand and I just sank to my knees to the ground and then forward on my face, a most extraordinary thing, and then after a little over on my back, I could never lie on my face for any length of time, much as I loved it, it made me feel sick, and lay there, half an hour perhaps, with my arms along my sides and the palms of my hands against the pebbles and my eyes wide open straying over the sky. Now was this my first experience of this kind, that is the question that immediately assails one. Falls I had had in plenty, of the kind after which unless a limb broken you pick yourself up and go on, cursing God and man, very different from this. With so much life gone from knowledge how know when all began, all the variants of the one that one by one their venom staling follow upon one another, all life long, till you succumb. So in some way even olden things each time are first things, no two breaths the same, all a going over and over and all once and never more. But let me get up now and on and get this awful day over and on to the next. But what is the sense of going on with all this, there is none. Day after unremembered day until my mother's death, then in a new place soon old until my own. And when I come to this night here among the rocks with my two books and the strong starlight it will have passed from me and the day that went before, my two books, the little and the big, all past and gone, or perhaps just moments here and there still, this little sound perhaps now that I don't understand so that I gather up my things and go back into my hole, so bygone they can be told. Over, over, there is a soft place in my heart for all that is over, no, for the being over, I love the word, words have been my only loves, not many. Often all day long as I went along I have said it, and sometimes I would be saying vero, oh vero. Oh but for those awful fidgets I have always had I would have lived my life in a big empty echoing room with a big old pendulum clock, just listening and dozing, the case open so that I could watch the swinging, moving my eyes to and fro, and the lead weights dangling lower and lower till I got up out of my chair and wound them up again, once a week. The third day was the look I got from the roadman, suddenly I see that now, the ragged old brute bent double down in the ditch leaning on his spade or whatever it was and leering round and up at me from under the brim of his slouch, the red mouth, how is it I wonder I saw him at all, that is more like it, the day I saw the look I got from Balfe, I went in terror of him as a child. Now he is dead and I resemble him. But let us get on and leave these old scenes and come to these, and my reward. Then it will not be as now, day after day, out, on, round, back, in, like leaves turning, or torn out and thrown crumpled away, but a long unbroken time without before or after, light or dark, from or towards or at, the old half knowledge of when and where gone, and of what, but kinds of things still, all at once, all going, until nothing, there was never anything, never can be, life and death all nothing, that kind of thing, only a voice dreaming and droning on all around, that is something, the voice that once was in your mouth. Well once out on the road and free of the property what then, I really do not know, the next thing I was up in the bracken lashing about with my stick making the drops fly and cursing, filthy language, the same words over and over, I hope nobody heard me. Throat very bad, to swallow was torment, and something wrong with an ear, I kept poking at it without relief, old wax perhaps pressing on the drum. Extraordinary still over the land, and in me too all quite still, a coincidence, why the curses were pouring out of me I do not know, no, that is a foolish thing to say, and the lashing about with the stick, what possessed me mild and weak to be doing that, as I struggled along. Is it the stoats now, no, first I just sink down again and disappear in the ferns, up to my waist they were as I went along. Harsh things these great ferns, like starched, very woody, terrible stalks, take the skin off your legs through your trousers, and then the holes they hide, break your leg if you're not careful, awful English this, fall and vanish from view, you could lie there for weeks and no one hear you, I often thought of that up in the mountains, no, that is a foolish thing to say, just went on, my body doing its best without me.

Faux Départs

1

Plus signe de vie, dites-vous, dis-je, bah, qu'à cela ne tienne,
imagination pas morte, et derechef, plus fort, trop fort,
Imagination pas morte, et le soir même m'enfermai sous les
huées et m'y mis, sans autre appui que les Syntaxes de Jolly et de
Draeger.
Mon cabinet a ceci de particulier, ou plutôt moi, que j'y ai fait
aménager une stalle à ma taille. C'est là, au fond, face au mur,
dans la pénombre, que j'imagine, tantôt assis, tantôt debout, au
besoin à genoux.
Dois-je me présenter? Bah.

2

Plus signe de vie, dis-tu, dis-je, bah, imagination pas morte.
Stalle, un mètre sur trois. C'est là. Par terre les Lexiques de Jolly
et de Draeger. J'éteins. C'est là, dans le fond, nez au mur.
Debout, assis, à genoux, selon. Toute la nuit naturelle. Me
présenter? Bah. Nous tourbillonnons vers l'hiver, moi, mon coin
de terre. Si ça pouvait être tout sur moi enfin. Et seuls désormais
l'autre vide, le silence et le noir sans faille.

3

Le vieux je est revenu, ne sachant d'où, ne sachant où, dénué de
sens, inchangé.
Plus ou moins de syllabes, de virgules pour le souffle, un point
pour le grand souffle.
Petits pas pressés, le pied qui se pose vient de trop loin, le ferme
plus bas a trop loin à aller, il n'y a pas eu de chemin.
Il parle à part lui à la dernière personne, il se dit. Il est revenu, il
ne sait d'où, il ne sait où, il n'a pas eu de chemin.

Le pied se pose une dernière fois, l'autre monte le rejoindre, il est rendu. Il peut lâcher son bâton blanc, il n'y a plus de bons ni de méchants, et s'allonger.

4

Imagination dead imagine.
Imagine a place, that again.
Never ask another question.
Imagine a place, then someone in it, that again.
Crawl out of the frowsy deathbed and drag it to a place to die in.
Out of the door and down the road in the old hat and coat like after the war, no, not that again.
A closed space five foot square by six high, try for him there.
Couldn't have got in, can't get out, did get in, will get out, all right.
Stool, bare walls when the light comes on, women's faces on the walls when the light comes on.
In a corner when the light comes on tattered Syntaxes of Jolly and Draeger Praeger Draeger, all right.
Light off and let him be, sitting on the stool and talking to himself the last person.
Saying, Now here is he, no, Now he is here.
Try as well as sitting standing, walking, kneeling, crawling, lying, creeping, in the dark and the light.
Imagine light.
Imagine light.
No visible source, strong at full, spread all over, no shadow, all six planes shining the same, slow on, ten seconds to full, same off, try that.
Still his crown touches the ceiling, moving not.
Say a lifetime of walking crouched and drawing himself up when brought to a stand.
When it goes out no matter, start again, another place, someone in it, keep glaring, never see, never find, no end, no matter.

All Strange Away

Imagination dead imagine. A place, that again. Never another question. A place, then someone in it, that again. Crawl out of the frowsy deathbed and drag it to a place to die in. Out of the door and down the road in the old hat and coat like after the war, no, not that again. Five foot square, six high, no way in, none out, try for him there. Stool, bare walls when the light comes on, women's faces on the walls when the light comes on. In a corner when the light comes on tattered syntaxes of Jolly and Draeger Praeger Draeger, all right. Light off and let him be, on the stool, talking to himself in the last person, murmuring, no sound, Now where is he, no, Now he is here. Sitting, standing, walking, kneeling, crawling, lying, creeping, in the dark and in the light, try all. Imagine light. Imagine light. No visible source, glare at full, spread all over, no shadow, all six planes shining the same, slow on, ten seconds on earth to full, same off, try that. Still his crown touches the ceiling, moving not, say a lifetime of walking bowed and full height when brought to a stand. It goes out, no matter, start again, another place, someone in it, keep glaring, never see, never find, no end, no matter. He says, no sound, The longer he lives and so the further goes the smaller they grow, the reasoning being the fuller he fills the space and so on, and the emptier, same reasoning. Hell this light from nothing no reason any moment, take off his coat, no, naked, all right, leave it for the moment. Sheets of black paper, stick them to the wall with cobweb and spittle, no good, shine like the rest. Imagine what needed, no more, any given moment, needed no more, gone, never was. Light flows, eyes close, stay closed till it ebbs, no, can't do that, eyes stay open, all right, look at that later. Black bag over his head, no good, all the rest still in light, front, sides, back, between the legs. Black shroud, start search for pins. Light on, down on knees, sights pin, makes for it, light out, gets pin in dark, light on, sights another, light out, so on, years of time on earth. Back on the stool in the shroud saying, That's better, now he's better, and so sits and never stirs, clutching it to him where it gapes, till it all perishes and rots off of him and hangs off of him in black flitters. Light out, long dark, candle and matches, imagine them, strike one to light, light on, blow out, light out, strike another, light on, so on. Light out, strike one to light, light on, light all the same, candlelight in light, blow out, light out, so on. No candle, no matches, no need, never were. As he was, in the dark any length, then the light when it flows till it ebbs any length, then again, so on, sitting, standing, walking, kneeling, crawling, lying, creeping, all any length, no paper, no pins, no candle, no matches, never were, talking to himself no sound in the last person any length, five foot square, six high, all white when light at full, no way in, none out. Falling on his knees in the dark to murmur, no sound, Fancy is his only hope. Surprised by light in this posture, hope and fancy on his lips, crawling lifelong habit to a corner here shadowless and similarly sinking head to ground here shining back into his eyes. Imagine eyes burnt ashen blue and lashes gone, lifetime of unseeing glaring, jammed open, one lightning wince per minute on earth, try that. Have him say, no sound, No way in, none out, he's not here. Tighten it round him, three foot square, five high, no stool, no sitting, no kneeling, no lying, just room to stand and revolve, light as before, faces as before, syntaxes upended in opposite corners. The back of his head touches the ceiling, say a lifetime of standing bowed. Call floor angles deasil, a, b, c and d and ceiling likewise e, f, g and h, say Jolly at b and Draeger at d, lean him for rest with feet at a and head at g, in dark and light, eyes glaring, murmuring, He's not here, no sound, Fancy is his only hope. Physique, flesh and fell, nail him to that while still tender, nothing clear, place again. Light as before, all white still when at full, flaking plaster or the like, floor like bleached dirt, aha. Faces now naked bodies, eye level, two per wall, eight in all, all right, details later. All six planes hot when shining, aha. So dark and cold any length, shivering more or less, feeble slaps want of room at all flesh within reach, little stamps of hampered feet, so on. Same system light and heat with sweat more or less, cringing away from walls, burning soles, now one, now the other. Murmur unaffected, He's not here, no sound, Fancy dead, gaping eyes unaffected. See how light stops at five soft and mild for bodies, eight no more, one per wall, four in all, say all of Emma. First face alone, lovely beyond words, leave it at that, then deasil breasts alone, then thighs and cunt alone, then arse and hole alone, all lovely beyond words. See how he crouches down and back to see, back of head against face when eyes on cunt, against breasts when on hole, and vice versa, all most clear. So in this soft and mild, crouched down and back with hands on knees to hold himself together, say deasil first from face through hole then back through face, murmuring, Imagine him kissing, caressing, licking, sucking, fucking and buggering all this stuff, no sound. Then halt and up to position of rest, back of head touching the ceiling, gaze on ground, lifetime of unbloody bowed unseeing glaring. Imagine lifetime, gems, evenings with Emma and the flights by night, no, not that again. Physique, too soon, perhaps never, vague bowed body bonewhite when light at full, nothing clear but ashen glare as imagined, no, attitudes too with play of joints most clear more various now. For nine and nine eighteen that is four feet and more across in which to kneel, arse on heels, hands on thighs, trunk best bowed and crown on ground. And even sit, knees drawn up, trunk best bowed, head between knees, arms round knees to hold all together. And even lie, arse to knees say diagonal ac, feet say at d, head on left cheek at b. Price to pay and highest lying more flesh touching glowing ground. But say not glowing enough to burn and turning over, see how that works. Arse to knees, say bd, feet say at c, head on right cheek at a. Then arse to knees say again ac, but feet at b and head on left cheek at d. Then arse to knees say again bd, but feet at a and head on right cheek at c. So on other four possibilities when begin again. All that most clear. Imaginable too flat on back, knees drawn up, hands holding shins to hold all together, glare

75

on ceiling, whereas flat on face by no stretch. Place then most clear so far but of him nothing and perhaps never save jointed segments variously disposed white when light at full. And always there among them somewhere the glaring eyes now clearer still in that flashes of vision few and far now rive their unseeingness. So for example as chance may have it on the ceiling a flyspeck or the insect itself or a strand of Emma's motte. Then lost and all the remaining field for hours of time on earth. Imagination dead imagine to lodge a second in that glare a dying common house of dying window fly, then fall the five feet to the dust and die or die and fall. No, no image, no fly here, no life or dying here but his, a speck of dirt. Or hers since sex not seen so far, say Emma standing, turning, sitting, kneeling, lying, in dark and light, saying to herself, She's not here, no sound, Fancy is her only hope, and Emmo on the walls, first the face, handsome beyond words, then deasil details later. And how crouching down and back she turns murmuring, Fancy her being all kissed, licked, sucked, fucked and so on by all that, no sound, hands on knees to hold herself together. Till halt and up, no, no image, down, for her down, to sit or kneel, kneel, arse on heels, hands on thighs, trunk bowed, breasts hanging, crown on ground, eyes glaring, no, no image, eyes closed, long lashes black when light, no more glare, never was, long black hair strewn when light, murmuring, no sound, Fancy dead. Any length, in dark and light, then topple left, arse to knees say db, feet say at c, head on left cheek at a, left breast puckered in the dust, hands, imagine hands. Imagine hands. Let her lie so from now on, have always lain so, head on left cheek in black hair at a and the rest the only way, never sat, never knelt, never stood, no Emmo, no need, never was. Imagine hands. Left on ball of right shoulder holding enough not to slip, right lightly clenched on ground, something in this hand, imagine later, something soft, clench tight, then lax and still any length, then tight again, so on, imagine later. Highest point from ground top of swell of right haunch, say twenty inches, slim woman. Ceiling wrong now, down two foot, perfect cube now, three foot every way, always was, light as before, all bonewhite

76

when at full as before, floor like bleached dirt, something there, leave it for the moment. Waste height, sixteen inches, strange, say some reason unimaginable now, imagine later, imagination dead imagine all strange away. Jolly and Draeger gone, never were. So far then hollow cube three foot overall, no way in imagined yet, none out. Black cold any length, then light slow up to full glare say ten seconds still and hot glare any length all ivory white all six planes no shadow, then down through deepening greys and gone, so on. Walls and ceiling flaking plaster or suchlike, floor like bleached dirt, aha, something there, leave if for the moment. Call floor angles deasil a, b, c and d and in here Emma lying on her left side, arse to knees along diagonal db with arse toward d and knees towards b though neither at either because too short and waste space here too some reason yet to be imagined. On left side then arse to knees db and consequently arse to crown along wall da though not flush because arse out with head on left cheek at a and remaining segment knees to feet along bc not flush because knees out with feet at c. In dark and light. Slow fade of ivory flesh when ebb ten seconds and gone. Long black hair when light strewn over face and adjacent floor. Uncover right eye and cheekbone vivid white for long black lashes when light. Say again though no real image puckered tip of left breast, leave right a mere name. Left hand clinging to right shoulder ball, right more faint loose fist on ground till fingers tighten as though to squeeze, imagine later, then loose again and still any length, so on. Murmuring, no sound, though say lips move with faint stir of hair, whether none emitted or air too rare, Fancy is her only hope, or, She's not here, or, Fancy dead, suggesting moments of discouragement, imagine other murmurs. In dark and light, no, dark alone, say murmurs now in dark alone as though in light all ears all six planes all ears when shining whereas in dark unheard, this a well-known thing. And yet no sound, well say a sound too faint for mortal ear. Imagine other murmurs. So great need of words not daring till at last slow ebb ten seconds, too fast, thirty now, great need not daring till at last slow ebb thirty seconds on earth through a thousand darkening greys till out and incontinent, Fancy dead, for instance if spirits low, no sound. But see how the light dies down and from half down or more slop up again to full and the words down again that were trembling up, all right, say mere delay, dark must be in the end, say dark and light here equal in the end that is when all done with dead imagining and measures taken dark and light seen equal in the end. And indeed how stay of flow or ebb at any grey any length and even on the very sill of black any length till at last in and black and at long last the murmur too faint for mortal ear. But murmurs in long dark so long that longing no but need for light as in long light for dark murmurs sometimes as great a space apart as from on earth a winter to a summer day and coming on that great silence, She's not here, for instance if in better spirits or, Fancy is her only hope, too faint for mortal ear. And other times to imagine other extreme so hard on one another any order and sometimes when all spent if not assuaged a second time in some quite different so run together that a mere torrent of hope and unhope mingled and submission amounting to nothing, get all this clearer later. Imagine other murmurs, Mother mother, Mother in heaven, Mother of God, God in heaven, combinations with Christ and Jesus, other proper names in great numbers say of loved ones for the most part and cherished haunts, imagine as needed, unsupported interjections, ancient Greek philosophers ejaculated with place of origin when possible suggesting pursuit of knowledge at some period, completed propositions such as, She is not here, the exception, imagine others, This is not possible, there is one, and here another of exceptional length, In a hammock in the sun and here the name of some bewitching site she lies sleeping. But sudden gleam that whatever words given to let fall soundless in the dark that if no sound better none, all right, try sound and if no better say quite speechless, imagine sound and not till then all that black hair toss back into the corner baring face as about to when this happened. Quite audible then now for her and if other ears there with her in the dark for them and if ears low down in the wall at a for them a voice without meaning, hear that. Then further quite expressionless, ohs and ahs copulate cold and no more feeling apparently in hammock than in Jesus Christ Almighty. And finally for the moment and then that face the tailaway so common in untrained speakers leaving sometimes in some doubt such things as which Diogenes and what fancy her only. Such then the sound roughly and if no clearer so then all the storm unspoken and the silence unbroken unless sound of light and dark or at the moments of change a sound of flow thirty seconds till full then silence any length till sound of ebb thirty seconds till black then silence any length, that might repay hearing and she hearing open then her eyes to lightening or darkening greys and not close them then to keep them closed till next sound of change till full light or dark, that might well be imagined. But at the same time say here all sound most doubtful though still too soon to deny and that in the end that is when all gone from mind and all mind gone that then none ever been but only silent flesh unless with the faint rise and fall of breast the breath to whip up to a pant if too faint alone and all others denied but still too soon. Hollow cube then three foot overall, full glare, head on left cheek in angle a and the rest the only way and say though no clear image now the long black hair now scattered clear of face on floor so clear when strewn on face now gone some reason, come back to that later, and on the face now bare all the glare for the moment. Gone the remembered long black lashes vivid white so clear before through gap in hair before all tossed back and lost some reason and face quite bare suggesting perhaps confusion then with errant threads of hair itself confused then with long lashes and so gone with hair or some other reason now quite gone. Cease here from face a space to note how place no longer cube but rotunda three foot diameter eighteen inches high supporting a dome semi-circular in section as in the Pantheon at Rome or certain beehive tombs and consequently three foot from ground to vertex that is at its highest point no lower than before with loss of floor space in the neighbourhood of two square feet or six square inches per lost angle and consequences for recumbent readily imaginable and of cubic an even higher figure, all right, resume face. But a, b, c and d now where any pair of right-angled diameters meet circumference meaning tighter fit for Emma with loss if folded as before of nearly one foot from crown to arse and of more than one from arse to knees and of nearly one from knees to feet though she still might be mathematically speaking more than seven foot long and merely a question of refolding in such a way that if head on left cheek at new a and feet at new c then arse no longer at new d but somewhere between it and new c and knees no longer at new b but somewhere between it and new a with segments angled more acutely that is head almost touching knees and feet almost touching arse, all that most clear. Rotunda then three foot diameter and three from ground to vertex, full glare, head on left cheek at a no longer new, when suddenly clear these dimensions faulty and small woman scarce five foot fully extended making rotunda two foot diameter and two from ground to vertex, full glare, face on left cheek at a and long segment that is from crown to arse now necessarily along diagonal too hastily assigned to middle with result face on left cheek with crown against wall at a and no longer feet but *arse* against wall at c there being no alternative and knees against wall ab a few inches from face and feet against wall bc a few inches from arse there being no alternatives and in this way the body tripled or trebled up and wedged in the only possible way in one half of the available room leaving the other empty, aha.

Diagram

Arms and hands as before for the moment. Rotunda then two foot across and at its highest two foot high, full glare, face on left cheek at a, long black hair gone, long black lashes on white cheekbone gone, glare from above for features on this bonewhite undoubted face right profile still hungering for missing lashes burning down for commisure of lids at least when like say without hesitation hell gaping they part and the black eye appears, leave now this face for the moment. Glare now on

hands most womanly clear and womanly especially right still
loosely clenched as before but no longer on ground since corrected pose but now on outer of right knee just where it swells to
thigh while left still loosely hitched to right shoulder ball as
before. All that most clear. That black eye still yawning before
going down to former to see what all this squeezing note how
the other slips a little way down slope of upper arm then back up
to ball, imagine squeeze again. Loose clench any length then
crush down most womanly straining knuckles five seconds then
back lax any length, all right, now down while fingers loose and
in between tips and palm that tiny chink, full glare all this time.
No real image but say like red no grey say like something grey
and when again squeeze firm down five seconds say faint hiss
then silence then back loose two seconds and say faint pop
and so arrive though no true image at small grey punctured
rubber ball or small grey ordinary rubber bulb such as on earth
attached to bottle of scent or suchlike that when squeezed a
jet of scent but here alone. So little by little all strange away.
Avalanche white lava mud seethe lid over eye permitting return
to face of which finally only that it could be nothing else, all
right. Thence on to neck in health by nature blank chunk nearer
to healthy natural neck with even hint of jugular and cords suggesting perhaps past her best and thence on down to other meat
when suddenly when least expected all this prying pointless and
enough for the moment and perhaps for ever this place so clear
now when light at full and this body hinged and crooked as
only the human man or woman living or not when light at full
without all this poking and prying about for cracks holes and
appendages. Rotunda then as before no change for the moment
in dark and light no visible source spread even no shadow slow
on thirty seconds to full same off to black two foot high at highest six and a half round good measure, wall peeling plaster or the
like supporting dome semi-circular in section same surface,
floor bleached dirt or similar, head wedged against wall at a with
blank face on left cheek and the rest the only way that is arse
wedged against wall at c and knees wedged against wall ab a few

inches from face and feet wedged against wall bc a few inches from arse, puckered tip of left breast no real image but maintain for the moment, left hand most clear and womanly lightly clasping right shoulder ball so lightly that slip from time to time down slope of right upper arm then back up to clasp, right no less on upper outer right knee lightly clasping any length small grey rubber sprayer bulb or grey punctured rubber ball then squeeze five seconds on earth faint hiss relax two seconds and pop or not, black right eye like maintain hell gaping any length then seethe of lid to cover imagine frequency later and motive, left also at same time or not or never imagine later, all contained in one hemicycle leaving other vacant, aha. All that if not yet quite complete quite clear and little change likely unless perhaps to complete unless perhaps somehow light sudden gleam perhaps better fixed and all this flowing and ebbing to full and empty more harm than good and better unchanging black or glare one or the other or between the two soft white unchanging but leave for the moment as seen from outset and never doubted slow on and off thirty seconds to glare and black any length through slow lightening and darkening greys from nothing for no reason yet imagined. Sleep stirring now some time add now with nightmares unimaginable making waking sweet and lying waking till longing for sleep again with dread of demons, perhaps some glimpse of demons later. Dread then in rotunda now with longing and sweet relief but so faint and weak no more than weak tremors of a hothouse leaf. Memories of past felicity no save one faint with faint ripple of sorrow of a lying side by side, look at this closer later. Imagine turning over with help of hinge of neck to bow head towards breast and so temporarily shorten long segment unwedging crown and arse with play enough to writhe till finally head wedged against wall at a as before but on right cheek and arse against wall at c as before but on right cheek and knees against wall a few inches from face as before but wall ad and feet against wall a few inches from arse as before but wall cd and so all tripled up and wedged as before but on the other side to rest the other and within the other hemicycle leaving the

82

other vacant, aha, all that most clear. Clear further how at some
earlier more callow stage this writhe again and again in vain
through weakness or natural awkwardness or want of pliancy or
want of resolution and how halfway through on back with legs
just clear how after some time in the balance thus the fall back
to where she lay head wedged against wall at a with blank face
on left cheek and arse against wall at c and knees against wall ab
and feet against wall bc with left hand clutching lightly right
shoulder ball and right on upper outer knee small grey sprayer
bulb or grey punctured rubber ball with disappointment naturally tinged perhaps with relief and this again and again till final
renouncement with faint sweet relief, faint disappointment will
have been here too. Sleep if maintained with cacodemons making waking in light and dark if this maintained faint sweet relief
and the longing for it again and to be gone again a folly to be
resisted again in vain. No memories of felicity save with faint
ripple of sorrow of a lying side by side and of misfortune none,
look closer later. So in rotunda up to now with disappointment
and relief with dread and longing sorrow all so weak and faint
no more than faint tremors of a leaf indoors on earth in winter
to survive till spring. Glare back now where all no light immeas-
urable turmoil no sound black soundless storm of which on
earth all being well say one millionth stilled to mean and of that
as much again by the more fortunate all being well vented as
only humans can. All gone now and never been never stilled
never voiced all back whence never sundered unstillable turmoil
no sound, She's not here, Fancy is her only, Mother mother,
Mother in heaven and of God, God in heaven, Christ and Jesus
all combinations, loved ones and places, philosophers and all
mere cries, In a hammock etc. and all such, leaving only for the
moment, Fancy dead, try that again with spirant barely parting
lips in murmur and faint stir of white dust or not in light and
dark if this maintained or dark alone as though ears when shining and dead uncertain in dying fall of amateur soliloquy when
not known for certain. Last look oh not farewell but last for
now on left side tripled up and wedged in half the room head

against wall at a and arse against wall at c and knees against wall ab an inch or so from head and feet against wall bc an inch or so from arse. Then look away then back for left hand clasping lightly right shoulder ball any length till slip and back to clasp and right on upper outer knee any length grey sprayer bulb or small grey punctured rubber ball till squeeze with hiss and loose again with pop or not. Long black hair and lashes gone and puckered breast no details to add to these for the moment save normal neck with hint of cords and jugular and black bottomless eye. Within apart from fancy dead and with faint sorrow faint memory of a lying side by side and in sleep demons not yet imagined all dark unappeasable turmoil no sound and so exhaled only for the moment with faint sound, Fancy dead, to which now add for old mind's sake sorrow vented in simple sighing sound black vowel a and further so that henceforth here no other sounds than these say gone now and never were sprayer bulb or punctured rubber ball and nothing ever in that hand lightly closed on nothing any length till for no reason yet imagined fingers tighten then relax no sound and to the same end slip of left hand down slope of right upper arm no sound and same purpose none of breath to the end that here henceforth no other sounds than these and never were that is than sop to mind faint sighing sound for tremor of sorrow at faint memory of a lying side by side and fancy murmured dead.

Imagination Dead Imagine

No trace anywhere of life, you say, pah, no difficulty there, imagination not dead yet, yes, dead, good, imagination dead imagine. Islands, waters, azure, verdure, one glimpse and vanished, endlessly, omit. Till all white in the whiteness the rotunda. No way in, go in, measure. Diameter three feet, three feet from ground to summit of the vault. Two diameters at right angles AB CD divide the white ground into two semicircles ACB BDA. Lying on the ground two white bodies, each in its semicircle. White too the vault and the round wall eighteen inches high from which it springs. Go back out, a plain rotunda, all white in the whiteness, go back in, rap, solid throughout, a ring as in the imagination the ring of bone. The light that makes all so white no visible source, all shines with the same white shine, ground, wall, vault, bodies, no shadow. Strong heat, surfaces hot but not burning to the touch, bodies sweating. Go back out, move back, the little fabric vanishes, ascend, it vanishes, all white in the whiteness, descend, go back in. Emptiness, silence, heat, whiteness, wait, the light goes down, all grows dark together, ground, wall, vault, bodies, say twenty seconds, all the greys, the light goes out, all vanishes. At the same time the temperature goes down, to reach its minimum, say freezing-point, at the same instant that the black is reached, which may seem strange. Wait, more or less long, light and heat come back, all grows white and hot together, ground, wall, vault, bodies, say twenty seconds, all the greys, till the initial level is reached whence the fall began. More or less long, for there may intervene, experience shows, between end of fall and beginning of rise, pauses of varying length, from the fraction of the second to what would have seemed, in other times, other places, an eternity. Same remark for the other pause, between end of rise and beginning of fall. The extremes, as long as they last, are perfectly stable, which in the case of the temperature may seem strange, in the beginning. It is possible too, experience shows, for rise and fall to stop short at any point and mark a pause, more or less long, before resuming, or reversing, the rise now fall, the fall rise, these in their turn to be completed, or to stop short and mark a pause, more or less long, before resuming, or again reversing, and so on, till finally one or the other extreme is reached. Such variations of rise and fall, combining in countless rhythms, commonly attend the passage from white and heat to black and cold, and vice versa. The extremes alone are stable, as is stressed by the vibration to be observed when a pause occurs at some intermediate stage, no matter what its level and duration. Then all vibrates, ground, wall, vault, bodies, ashen or leaden or between the two, as may be. But on the whole, experience shows, such uncertain passage is not common. And most often, when the light begins to fail, and along with it the heat, the movement continues unbroken until, in the space of some twenty seconds, pitch black is reached and at the same instant say freezing-point. Same remark for the reverse movement, towards heat and whiteness. Next most frequent is the fall or rise with pauses of varying length in these feverish greys, without at any moment reversal of the movement. But whatever its uncertainties the return sooner or later to a temporary calm seems assured, for the moment, in the black dark or the great whiteness, with attendant temperature, world still proof against enduring tumult. Rediscovered miraculously after what absence in perfect voids it is no longer quite the same, from this point of view, but there is no other. Externally all is as before and the sighting of the little fabric quite as much a matter of chance, its whiteness merging in the surrounding whiteness. But go in and now briefer lulls and never twice the same storm. Light and heat remain linked as though supplied by the same source of which still no trace. Still on the ground, bent in three, the head against the wall at B, the arse against the wall at A, the knees against the wall between B and C, the feet against the wall between C and A, that is to say inscribed in the semicircle ACB, merging in the white ground were it not for the long hair of strangely imperfect whiteness, the white body of a woman finally. Similarly inscribed in the other semicircle, against the wall his head at A, his arse at B, his knees between A and D, his feet between D and B, the partner. On their right sides therefore both and back to back head to arse. Hold a mirror to their lips, it mists. With their left hands they hold their left legs a little below the knee, with their right hands their left arms a little above the elbow. In this agitated light, its great white calm now so rare and brief, inspection is not easy. Sweat and mirror notwithstanding they might well pass for inanimate but for the left eyes which at incalculable intervals suddenly open wide and gaze in unblinking exposure long beyond what is humanly possible. Piercing pale blue the effect is striking, in the beginning. Never the two gazes together except once, when the beginning of one overlapped the end of the other, for about ten seconds. Neither fat nor thin, big nor small, the bodies seem whole and in fairly good condition, to judge by the surfaces exposed to view. The faces too, assuming the two sides of a piece, seem to want nothing essential. Between their absolute stillness and the convulsive light the contrast is striking, in the beginning, for one who still remembers having been struck by the contrary. It is clear however, from a thousand little signs too long to imagine, that they are not sleeping. Only murmur ah, no more, in this silence, and at the same instant for the eye of prey the infinitesimal shudder instantaneously suppressed. Leave them there, sweating and icy, there is better elsewhere. No, life ends and no, there is nothing elsewhere, and no question now of ever finding again that white speck lost in whiteness, to see if they still lie still in the stress of that storm, or of a worse storm, or in the black dark for good, or the great whiteness unchanging, and if not what they are doing.

Enough

All that goes before forget. Too much at a time is too much. That gives the pen time to note. I don't see it but I hear it there behind me. Such is the silence. When the pen stops I go on. Sometimes it refuses. When it refuses I go on. Too much silence is too much. Or it's my voice too weak at times. The one that comes out of me. So much for the art and craft.

I did all he desired. I desired it too. For him. Whenever he desired something so did I. He only had to say what thing. When he didn't desire anything neither did I. In this way I didn't live without desires. If he had desired something for me I would have desired it too. Happiness for example or fame. I only had the desires he manifested. But he must have manifested them all. All his desires and needs. When he was silent he must have been like me. When he told me to lick his penis I hastened to do so. I drew satisfaction from it. We must have had the same satisfactions. The same needs and the same satisfactions.

One day he told me to leave him. It's the verb he used. He must have been on his last legs. I don't know if by that he meant me to leave him for good or only to step aside a moment. I never asked myself the question. I never asked myself any questions but his. Whatever it was he meant I made off without looking back. Gone from reach of his voice I was gone from his life. Perhaps it was that he desired. There are questions you see and don't ask yourself. He must have been on his last legs. I on the contrary was far from on my last legs. I belonged to an entirely different generation. It didn't last. Now that I'm entering night I have kinds of gleams in my skull. Stony ground but not entirely. Given three or four lives I might have accomplished something.

I cannot have been more than six when he took me by the hand. Barely emerging from childhood. But it didn't take me long to emerge altogether. It was the left hand. To be on the right was more than he could bear. We advanced side by side hand in hand. One pair of gloves was enough. The free or outer hands hung bare. He did not like to feel against his skin the skin of another. Mucous membrane is a different matter. Yet he sometimes took off his glove. Then I had to take off mine. We would cover in this way a hundred yards or so linked by our bare extremities. Seldom more. That was enough for him. If the question were put to me I would say that odd hands are ill-fitted for intimacy. Mine never felt at home in his. Sometimes they let each other go. The clasp loosened and they fell apart. Whole minutes often passed before they clasped again. Before his clasped mine again.

They were cotton gloves rather tight. Far from blunting the shapes they sharpened them by simplifying. Mine was naturally too loose for years. But it didn't take me long to fill it. He said I had Aquarius hands. It's a mansion above.

All I know comes from him. I won't repeat this apropos of all my bits of knowledge. The art of combining is not my fault. It's a curse from above. For the rest I would suggest not guilty.

Our meeting. Though very bowed already he looked a giant to me. In the end his trunk ran parallel with the ground. To counterbalance this anomaly he held his legs apart and sagged at the knees. His feet grew more and more flat and splay. His horizon was the ground they trod. Tiny moving carpet of turf and trampled flowers. He gave me his hand like a tired old ape with the elbow lifted as high as it would go. I had only to straighten up to be head and shoulders above him. One day he halted and fumbling for his words explained to me that anatomy is a whole.

In the beginning he always spoke walking. So it seems to me now. Then sometimes walking and sometimes still. In the end still only. And the voice getting fainter all the time. To save him having to say the same thing twice running I bowed right down. He halted and waited for me to get into position. As soon as out of the corner of his eye he glimpsed my head alongside his the murmurs came. Nine times out of ten they did not concern me.

But he wished everything to be heard including the ejaculations and broken paternosters that he poured out to the flowers at his feet.

He halted then and waited for my head to arrive before telling me to leave him. I snatched away my hand and made off without looking back. Two steps and I was lost to him for ever. We were severed if that is what he desired.

His talk was seldom of geodesy. But we must have covered several times the equivalent of the terrestrial equator. At an average speed of roughly three miles per day and night. We took flight in arithmetic. What mental calculations bent double hand in hand! Whole ternary numbers we raised in this way to the third power sometimes in downpours of rain. Graving themselves in his memory as best they could the ensuing cubes accumulated. In view of the converse operation at a later stage. When time would have done its work.

If the question were put to me suitably framed I would say yes indeed the end of this long outing was my life. Say about the last seven thousand miles. Counting from the day when alluding for the first time to his infirmity he said he thought it had reached its peak. The future proved him right. That part of it at least we were to make past of together.

I see the flowers at my feet and it's the others I see. Those we trod down with equal step. It is true they are the same.

Contrary to what I had long been pleased to imagine he was not blind. Merely indolent. One day he halted and fumbling for his words described his vision. He concluded by saying he thought it would get no worse. How far this was not a delusion I cannot say. I never asked myself the question. When I bowed down to receive his communications I felt on my eye a glint of blue bloodshot apparently affected.

He sometimes halted without saying anything. Either he had finally nothing to say or while having something to say he finally decided not to say it. I bowed down as usual to save him having to repeat himself and we remained in this position. Bent double heads touching silent hand in hand. While all about us fast on

95

one another the minutes flew. Sooner or later his foot broke away from the flowers and we moved on. Perhaps only to halt again after a few steps. So that he might say at last what was in his heart or decide not to say it again.

Other main examples suggest themselves to the mind. Immediate continuous communication with immediate redeparture. Same thing with delayed redeparture. Delayed continuous communication with immediate redeparture. Same thing with delayed redeparture. Immediate discontinuous communication with immediate redeparture. Same thing with delayed redeparture. Delayed discontinuous communication with immediate redeparture. Same thing with delayed redeparture.

It is then I shall have lived then or never. Ten years at the very least. From the day he drew the back of his left hand lingeringly over his sacral ruins and launched his prognostic. To the day of my supposed disgrace. I can see the place a step short of the crest. Two steps forward and I was descending the other slope. If I had looked back I would not have seen him.

He loved to climb and therefore I too. He clamoured for the steepest slopes. His human frame broke down into two equal segments. This thanks to the shortening of the lower by the sagging knees. On a gradient of one in one his head swept the ground. To what this taste was due I cannot say. To love of the earth and the flowers' thousand scents and hues. Or to cruder imperatives of an anatomical order. He never raised the question. The crest once reached alas the going down again.

In order from time to time to enjoy the sky he resorted to a little round mirror. Having misted it with his breath and polished it on his calf he looked in it for the constellations. I have it! he exclaimed referring to the Lyre or the Swan. And often he added that the sky seemed much the same.

We were not in the mountains however. There were times I discerned on the horizon a sea whose level seemed higher than ours. Could it be the bed of some vast evaporated lake or drained of its waters from below? I never asked myself the question.

The fact remains we often came upon this sort of mound some three hundred feet in height. Reluctantly I raised my eyes and discerned the nearest often on the horizon. Or instead of moving on from the one we had just descended we ascended it again.

I am speaking of our last decade comprised between the two events described. It veils those that went before and must have resembled it like blades of grass. To those engulfed years it is reasonable to impute my education. For I don't remember having learnt anything in those I remember. It is with this reasoning I calm myself brought up short by all I know.

I set the scene of my disgrace just short of a crest. On the contrary it was on the flat in a great calm. If I had looked back I would have seen him in the place where I had left him. Some trifle would have shown me my mistake if mistake there had been. In the years that followed I did not exclude the possibility of finding him again. In the place where I had left him if not elsewhere. Or of hearing him call me. At the same time telling myself he was on his last legs. But I did not count on it unduly. For I hardly raised my eyes from the flowers. And his voice was spent. And as if that were not enough I kept telling myself he was on his last legs. So it did not take me long to stop counting on it altogether.

I don't know what the weather is now. But in my life it was eternally mild. As if the earth had come to rest in spring. I am thinking of our hemisphere. Sudden pelting downpours overtook us. Without noticeable darkening of the sky. I would not have noticed the windlessness if he had not spoken of it. Of the wind that was no more. Of the storms he had ridden out. It is only fair to say there was nothing to sweep away. The very flowers were stemless and flush with the ground like water-lilies. No brightening our buttonholes with these.

We did not keep tally of the days. If I arrive at ten years it is thanks to our pedometer. Total mileage divided by average daily mileage. So many days. Divide. Such a figure the night before the sacrum. Such another the eve of my disgrace. Daily average always up to date. Subtract. Divide.

Night. As long as day in this endless equinox. It falls and we go on. Before dawn we are gone.

Attitude at rest. Wedged together bent in three. Second right angle at the knees. I on the inside. We turn over as one man when he manifests the desire. I can feel him at night pressed against me with all his twisted length. It was less a matter of sleeping than of lying down. For we walked in a half sleep. With his upper hand he held and touched me where he wished. Up to a certain point. The other was twined in my hair. He murmured of things that for him were no more and for me could not have been. The wind in the overground stems. The shade and shelter of the forests.

He was not given to talk. An average of a hundred words per day and night. Spaced out. A bare million in all. Numerous repeats. Ejaculations. Too few for even a cursory survey. What do I know of man's destiny? I could tell you more about radishes. For them he had a fondness. If I saw one I would name it without hesitation.

We lived on flowers. So much for sustenance. He halted and without having to stoop caught up a handful of petals. Then moved munching on. They had on the whole a calming action. We were on the whole calm. More and more. All was. This notion of calm comes from him. Without him I would not have had it. Now I'll wipe out everything but the flowers. No more rain. No more mounds. Nothing but the two of us dragging through the flowers. Enough my old breasts feel his old hand.

The Lost Ones

Abode where lost bodies roam each searching for its lost one. Vast enough for search to be in vain. Narrow enough for flight to be in vain. Inside a flattened cylinder fifty metres round and sixteen high for the sake of harmony. The light. Its dimness. Its yellowness. Its omnipresence as though every separate square centimetre were agleam of the some twelve million of total surface. Its restlessness at long intervals suddenly stilled like panting at the last. Then all go dead still. It is perhaps the end of their abode. A few seconds and all begins again. Consequences of this light for the searching eye. Consequences for the eye which having ceased to search is fastened to the ground or raised to the distant ceiling where none can be. The temperature. It oscillates with more measured beat between hot and cold. It passes from one extreme to the other in about four seconds. It too has its moments of stillness more or less hot or cold. They coincide with those of the light. Then all go dead still. It is perhaps the end of all. A few seconds and all begins again. Consequences of this climate for the skin. It shrivels. The bodies brush together with a rustle of dry leaves. The mucous membrane itself is affected. A kiss makes an indescribable sound. Those with stomach still to copulate strive in vain. But they will not give in. Floor and walls are of solid rubber or suchlike. Dash against them foot or fist or head and the sound is scarcely heard. Imagine then the silence of the steps. The only sounds worthy of the name result from the manipulation of the ladders or the thud of bodies striking against one another or of one against itself as when in sudden fury it beats its breast. Thus flesh and bone subsist. The ladders. These are the only objects. They are single without exception and vary greatly in size. The shortest measure not less than six metres. Some are fitted with a sliding extension. They are propped against the wall without regard to harmony. Bolt upright on the

101

top rung of the tallest the tallest climbers can touch the ceiling with their fingertips. Its composition is no less familiar therefore than that of floor and wall. Dash a rung against it and the sound is scarcely heard. These ladders are in great demand. At the foot of each at all times or nearly a little queue of climbers. And yet it takes courage to climb. For half the rungs are missing and this without regard to harmony. If only every second one were missing no great harm would be done. But the want of three in a row calls for acrobatics. These ladders are nevertheless in great demand and in no danger of being reduced to mere uprights runged at their extremities alone. For the need to climb is too widespread. To feel it no longer is a rare deliverance. The missing rungs are in the hands of a happy few who use them mainly for attack and self-defence. Their solitary attempts to brain themselves culminate at the best in brief losses of consciousness. The purpose of the ladders is to convey the searchers to the niches. Those whom these entice no longer climb simply to get clear of the ground. It is the custom not to climb two or more at a time. To the fugitive fortunate enough to find a ladder free it offers certain refuge until the clamours subside. The niches or alcoves. These are cavities sunk in that part of the wall which lies above an imaginary line running midway between floor and ceiling and features therefore of its upper half alone. A more or less wide mouth gives rapid access to a chamber of varying capacity but always sufficient for a body in reasonable command of its joints to enter in and similarly once in to crouch down after a fashion. They are disposed in irregular quincunxes roughly ten metres in diameter and cunningly out of line. Such harmony only he can relish whose long experience and detailed knowledge of the niches are such as to permit a perfect mental image of the entire system. But it is doubtful that such a one exists. For each climber has a fondness for certain niches and refrains as far as possible from the others. A certain number are connected by tunnels opened in the thickness of the wall and attaining in some cases no fewer than fifty metres in length. But most have no other way out than the way in. It is as though at a certain stage discouragement had prevailed. To be noted in support of this wild surmise the existence of a long tunnel abandoned blind. Woe the body that rashly enters here to be compelled finally after long efforts to crawl back backwards as best it can the way it came. Not that this drama is peculiar to the unfinished tunnel. One has only to consider what inevitably must ensue when two bodies enter a normal tunnel at the same time by opposite ends. Niches and tunnels are subject to the same light and climate as the rest of the abode. So much for a first aperçu of the abode.

One body per square metre or two hundred bodies in all round numbers. Whether relatives near and far or friends in varying degree many in theory are acquainted. The gloom and press make recognition difficult. Seen from a certain angle these bodies are of four kinds. Firstly those perpetually in motion. Secondly those who sometimes pause. Thirdly those who short of being driven off never stir from the coign they have won and when driven off pounce on the first free one that offers and freeze again. That is not quite accurate. For if among these sedentary the need to climb is dead it is none the less subject to strange resurrections. The quidam then quits his post in search of a free ladder or to join the nearest or shortest queue. The truth is that no searcher can readily forgo the ladder. Paradoxically the sedentary are those whose acts of violence most disrupt the cylinder's quiet. Fourthly those who do not search or non-searchers sitting for the most part against the wall in the attitude which wrung from Dante one of his rare wan smiles. By non-searchers and despite the abyss to which this leads it is finally impossible to understand other than ex-searchers. To rid this notion of some of its virulence one has only to suppose the need to search no less resurrectable than that of the ladder and those eyes to all appearances for ever cast down or closed possessed of the strange power suddenly to kindle again before passing face and body. But enough will always sub-sist to spell for this little people the extinction soon or late of its last remaining fires. A languishing happily unperceived because of its slowness and the resurgences that make up for it in part and the inattention of those concerned dazed by the passion preying on them still or by the state of languor into which imperceptibly they are already fallen. And far from being able to imagine their last state when every body will be still and every eye vacant they will come to it unwitting and be so unawares. Then light and climate will be changed in a way impossible to foretell. But the former may be imagined extinguished as purposeless and the latter fixed not far from freezing point. In cold darkness motionless flesh. So much roughly speaking for these bodies seen from a certain angle and for this notion and its consequences if it is maintained.

Inside a cylinder fifty metres round and sixteen high for the sake of harmony or a total surface of roughly twelve hundred square metres of which eight hundred mural. Not counting the niches and tunnels. Omnipresence of a dim yellow light shaken by a vertiginous tremolo between contiguous extremes. Temperature agitated by a like oscillation but thirty or forty times slower in virtue of which it falls rapidly from a maximum of twenty-five degrees approximately to a minimum of approximately five whence a regular variation of five degrees per second. That is not quite accurate. For it is clear that at both extremes of the shuttle the difference can fall to as little as one degree only. But this remission never lasts more than a little less than a second. At great intervals suspension of the two vibrations fed no doubt from a single source and resumption together after a lull of varying duration but never exceeding ten seconds or thereabouts. Corresponding abeyance of all motion among the bodies in motion and heightened fixity of the motionless. Only objects fifteen single ladders propped against the wall at irregular intervals. In the upper half of the wall disposed quincuncially for the sake of harmony a score of niches some connected by tunnels.

From time immemorial rumour has it or better still the notion is abroad that there exists a way out. Those who no longer believe so are not immune from believing so again in accordance with the notion requiring as long as it holds that here all should die but with so gradual and to put it plainly so fluctuant a death as to escape the notice even of a visitor. Regarding the nature of this way out and its location two opinions divide without opposing all those still loyal to that old belief. One school swears by a secret passage branching from one of the tunnels and leading in the words of the poet to nature's sanctuaries. The other dreams of a trapdoor hidden in the hub of the ceiling giving access to a flue at the end of which the sun and other stars would still be shining. Conversion is frequent either way and such a one who at a given moment would hear of nothing but the tunnel may well a moment later hear of nothing but the trapdoor and a moment later still give himself the lie again. The fact remains none the less that of these two persuasions the former is declining in favour of the latter but in a manner so desultory and slow and of course with so little effect on the comportment of either sect that to perceive it one must be in the secret of the gods. This shift has logic on its side. For those who believe in a way out possible of access as via a tunnel it would be and even without any thought of putting it to account may be tempted by its quest. Whereas the partisans of the trapdoor are spared this demon by the fact that the hub of the ceiling is out of reach. Thus by insensible degrees the way out transfers from the tunnel to the ceiling prior to never having been. So much for a first aperçu of this credence so singular in itself and by reason of the loyalty it inspires in the hearts of so many possessed. Its fatuous little light will be assuredly the last to leave them always assuming they are darkward bound.

Bolt upright on the top run of the great ladder fully extended and reared against the wall the tallest climbers can touch the edge of the ceiling with their fingertips. On the same ladder planted perpendicular at the centre of the floor the same bodies would gain half a metre and so be enabled to explore at leisure the fabulous zone decreed out of reach and which therefore in theory is in no wise so. For such recourse to the ladder is conceivable. All that is needed is a score of determined volunteers joining forces to keep it upright with the help if necessary of other ladders acting as stays or struts. An instant of fraternity.

But outside their explosions of violence this sentiment is as foreign to them as to butterflies. And this owing not so much to want of heart or intelligence as to the ideal preying on one and all. So much for this inviolable zenith where for amateurs of myth lies hidden a way out to earth and sky.

The use of the ladders is regulated by conventions of obscure origin which in their precision and the submission they exact from the climbers resemble laws. Certain infractions unleash against the culprit a collective fury surprising in creatures so peaceable on the whole and apart from the grand affair so careless of one another. Others on the contrary scarcely ruffle the general indifference. This at first sight is strange. All rests on the rule against mounting the ladder more than one at a time. It remains taboo therefore to the climber waiting at its foot until such time as his predecessor has regained the ground. Idle to imagine the confusion that would result from the absence of such a rule or from its non-observance. But devised for the convenience of all there is no question of its applying without restriction or as a licence for the unprincipled climber to engross the ladder beyond what is reasonable. For without some form of curb he might take the fancy to settle down permanently in one of the niches or tunnels leaving behind him a ladder out of service for good and all. And were others to follow his example as inevitably they must the spectacle would finally be offered of one hundred and eighty-five searchers less the vanquished committed for all time to the ground. Not to mention the intolerable presence of properties serving no purpose. It is therefore understood that after a certain interval difficult to assess but unerringly timed by all the ladder is again available meaning at the disposal in the same conditions of him due next to climb easily recognizable by his position at the head of the queue and so much the worst for the abuser. The situation of this latter having lost his ladder is delicate indeed and seems to exclude a priori his ever returning to the ground. Happily sooner or later he succeeds in doing so thanks to a further provision giving priority at all times to descent over ascent. He has therefore merely to watch at the mouth of his niche for a ladder to present itself and immediately start down quite easy in his mind knowing full well that whoever below is on the point of mounting if not already on his way up will give way in his favour. The worst that can befall him is a long vigil because of the ladders' mobility. It is indeed rare for a climber when it comes to his turn to content himself with the same niche as his predecessor and this for obvious reasons that will appear in due course. But rather he makes off with his ladder followed by the queue and plants it under one or other of the five niches available by reason of the difference in number between these and the ladders. But to return to the unfortunate having outstayed his time it is clear that his chances of rapid redescent will be increased though far from doubled if thanks to a tunnel he disposes of two niches from which to watch. Though even in this event he usually prefers and invariably if the tunnel is a long one to plump for one only lest a ladder should present itself at one or the other and he still crawling between the two. But the ladders do not serve only as vehicles to the niches and tunnels and those whom these have ceased if only temporarily to entice use them simply to get clear of the ground. They mount to the level of their choice and there stay and settle standing as a rule with their faces to the wall. This family of climbers too is liable to exceed the allotted time. It is in order then for him due next for the ladder to climb in the wake of the offender and by means of one or more thumps on the back bring him back to a sense of his surroundings. Upon which he unfailingly hastens to descend preceded by his successor who has then merely to take over the ladder subject to the usual conditions. This docility in the abuser shows clearly that the abuse is not deliberate but due to a temporary derangement of his inner timepiece easy to understand and therefore to forgive. Here is the reason why this in reality infrequent infringement whether on the part of those who push on up to the niches and tunnels or of those who halt on the way never gives rise to the fury vented on the wretch with no better sense than to climb before his time and yet whose precipitancy one would have thought quite as understandable and consequently forgivable as the converse excess. This is indeed strange. But what is at stake is the fundamental principle forbidding ascent more than one at a time the repeated violation of which would soon transform the abode into a pandemonium. Whereas the belated return to the ground hurts finally none but the laggard himself. So much for a first aperçu of the climbers' code.

Similarly the transport of the ladders is not left to the good pleasure of the carriers who are required to hug the wall at all times eddywise. This is a rule no less strict than the prohibition to climb more than one at a time and not lightly to be broken. Nothing more natural. For if for the sake of the shortcut it were permitted to carry the ladder slap through the press or skirting the wall at will in either direction life in the cylinder would soon become untenable. All along the wall therefore a belt about one metre wide is reserved for the carriers. To this zone those also are confined who wait their turn to climb and must close their ranks and flatten themselves as best they can with their backs to the wall so as not to encroach on the arena proper.

It is curious to note the presence within this belt of a certain number of sedentary searchers sitting or standing against the wall. Dead to the ladders to all intents and purposes and a source of annoyance for both climbers and carriers they are nevertheless tolerated. The fact is that these sort of semi-sages among whom all ages are to be admired from old age to infancy inspire in those still fitfully fevering if not a cult at least a certain deference. They cling to this as to a homage due to them and are morbidly susceptible to the least want of consideration. A sedentary searcher stepped on instead of over is capable of such an outburst of fury as to throw the entire cylinder into a ferment. Cleave also to the wall both sitting and standing four vanquished out of five. They may be walked on without their reacting.

To be noted finally the care taken by the searchers in the arena not to overflow on the climbers' territory. When weary of searching among the throng they turn towards this zone it is only to skirt with measured tread its imaginary edge devouring with their eyes its occupants. Their slow round counter-carrierwise creates a second even narrower belt respected in its turn by the main body of searchers. Which suitably lit from above would give the impression at times of two narrow rings turning in opposite directions about the teeming precinct.

One body per square metre of available surface or two hundred bodies in all round numbers. Bodies of either sex and all ages from old age to infancy. Sucklings who having no longer to suck huddle at gaze in the lap or sprawled on the ground in precocious postures. Others a little more advanced crawl searching among the legs. Picturesque detail a woman with white hair still young to judge by her thighs leaning against the wall with eyes closed in abandonment and mechanically clasping to her breast a mite who strains away in an effort to turn its head and look behind. But such tiny ones are comparatively few. None looks within himself where none can be. Eyes cast down or closed signify abandonment and are confined to the vanquished. These precisely to be counted on the fingers of one hand are not necessarily still. They may stray unseeing through the throng indistinguishable to the eye of flesh from the still unrelenting. These recognize them and make way. They may wait their turn at the foot of the ladders and when it comes ascend to the niches or simply leave the ground. They may crawl blindly in the tunnels in search of nothing. But normally abandonment freezes them both in space and in their pose whether standing or sitting as a rule profoundly bowed. It is this makes it possible to tell them from the sedentary devouring with their eyes in heads dead still each body as it passed by. Standing or sitting they cleave to the wall all but one in the arena stricken rigid in the midst of the fevering. These recognize him and keep their distance. The spent eyes may have fits of the old craving just as those who having renounced the ladder suddenly take to it again. So true it is that when in the cylinder what little is possible is not so it is merely no longer so and in the least less the all of nothing if this notion is maintained. Then the eyes suddenly start to search afresh as famished as the unthinkable first day until for no clear reason they as suddenly close again or the head falls. Even so a great heap of sand sheltered from the wind lessened by three grains every second year and every following increased by two if this notion is maintained. If then the vanquished have still some way to go what can be said of the others and what better name be given them than the fair name of searchers? Some and indeed by far the greater number never pause except when they line up for a ladder or watch out at the mouth of a niche. Some come to rest from time to time all but the unceasing eyes. As for the sedentary if they never stir from the coign they have won it is because they have calculated their best chance is there and if they seldom or never ascend to the niches and tunnels it is because they have done so too often in vain or come there too often to grief. An intelligence would be tempted to see in these the next vanquished and continuing in its stride to require of those still perpetually in motion that they all soon or late one after another be as those who sometimes pause and of these that they finally be as the sedentary and of the sedentary that they be in the end as the vanquished and of the two hundred vanquished thus obtained that all in due course each in his turn be well and truly vanquished for good and all each frozen in his place and attitude. But let these families be numbered in order of maturity and experience shows that it is possible to graduate from one to three skipping two and from one to four skipping two or three or both and from two to four skipping three. In the other direction the ill-vanquished may at long intervals and with each relapse more briefly revert to the state of the sedentary who in their turn count a few chronic waverers prone to succumb to the ladder again while remaining dead to the arena. But never again will they ceaselessly come and go who now at long intervals come to rest without ceasing to search with their eyes. In the beginning then unthinkable as the end all roamed without respite including the nurselings in so far as they were borne except of course those already at the foot of the ladders or frozen in the tunnels the better to listen or crouching all eyes in the niches and so roamed a vast space of time impossible to measure until a first came to a standstill followed by a second and so on. But as to at this moment of time and there will be no other numbering the faithful who endlessly come and go impatient of the least repose and those who every now and then stand still and the sedentary and the so-called vanquished may it suffice to state that at this moment of time to the nearest body in spite of the press and gloom the first are twice as many as the second who are three times as many as the third who are four times as many as the fourth namely five vanquished in all. Relatives and friends are well represented not to speak of mere acquaintances. Press and gloom make recognition difficult. Man and wife are strangers two paces apart to mention only this most intimate of bonds. Let them move on till they are close enough to touch and then without pausing on their way exchange a look. If they recognize each other it does not appear. Whatever it is they are searching for it is not that.

What first impresses in this gloom is the sensation of yellow it imparts not to say of sulphur in view of the associations. Then how it throbs with constant unchanging beat and fast but not so fast that the pulse is no longer felt. And finally much later that ever and anon there comes a momentary lull. The effect of those brief and rare respites is unspeakably dramatic to put it mildly. Those who never know a moment's rest stand rooted to the spot often in extravagant postures and the stillness heightened tenfold of the sedentary and vanquished makes that which is normally theirs seem risible in comparison. The fists on their way to smite in anger or discouragement freeze in their arcs until the scare is past and the blow can be completed or volley of blows. Similarly without entering into tedious details those surprised in the act of climbing or carrying a ladder or making unmakable love or crouched in the niches or crawling in the tunnels as the case may be. But a brief ten seconds at most and the throbbing is resumed and all is as before. Those interrupted in their coming and going start coming and going again and the motionless relax. The lovers buckle to anew and the fists carry on where they left off. The murmur cut off as though by a switch fills the cylinder again. Among all the components the sum of which it is the ear finally distinguishes a faint stridulence as of insects which is that of the light itself and the one invariable. Between the extremes that delimit the vibration the difference is of two or three candles at the most. So that the sensation of yellow is faintly tinged with one of red. Light in a word that not only dims but blurs into the bargain. It might safely be maintained that the eye grows used to these conditions and in the end adapts to them were it not that just the contrary is to be observed in the slow deterioration of vision ruined by this fiery flickering murk and by the incessant straining for ever vain with concomitant moral distress and its repercussion on the organ. And were it possible to follow over a long enough period of time eyes blue for preference as being the most perishable they would be seen to redden more and more in an ever widening glare and their pupils little by little to dilate till the whole orb was devoured. And all by such slow and insensible degrees to be sure as to pass unperceived even by those most concerned if this notion is maintained. And the thinking being coldly intent on all these data and evidences could scarcely escape at the close of his analysis the mistaken conclusion that instead of speaking of the vanquished with the slight taint of pathos attaching to the term it would be more correct to speak of the blind and leave it at that. Once the first shocks of surprise are finally past this light is further unusual in that far from evincing one or more visible or hidden sources it appears to emanate from all sides and to permeate the entire space as though this were uniformly luminous down to its least particle of ambient air. To the point that the ladders themselves seem rather to shed than to receive light with this slight reserve that light is not the word. No other shadows then than those cast by the bodies pressing on one another wilfully or from necessity as when for example on a breast to prevent its being lit or on some private part the hand descends with vanished palm. Whereas the skin of a climber alone on his ladder or in the depths of a tunnel glistens all over with the same red-yellow glister and even some of its folds and recesses in so far as the air enters in. With regard to the temperature its oscillation is between much wider extremes and at a much lower frequency since it takes not less than four seconds to pass from its minimum of five degrees to its maximum of twenty-five and inversely namely an average of only five degrees per second. Does this mean that with every passing second there is a rise or fall of five degrees exactly neither more nor less? Not quite. For it is clear there are two periods in the scale namely from twenty-one degrees on on the way up and from nine on on the way down when this difference will not be reached. Out of the eight seconds therefore required for a single rise and fall it is only during a bare six and a half that the bodies suffer the maximum increment of heat or cold which with the help of a little addition or better still division works out nevertheless at some twenty years respite per century in this domain. There is something disturbing at first sight in the relative slowness of this vibration compared to that of the light. But this is a disturbance analysis makes short work of. For on due reflection the difference to be considered is not one of speed but of space travelled. And if that required of the temperature were reduced to the equivalent of a few candles there would be nothing to choose mutatis mutandis between the two effects. But that would not answer the needs of the cylinder. So all is for the best. The more so as the two storms have this in common that when one is cut off as though by magic then in the same breath the other also as though again the two were connected somewhere to a single commutator. For in the cylinder alone are certitudes to be found and without nothing but mystery. At vast intervals then the bodies enjoy ten seconds at most of unbroken warmth or cold or between the two. But this cannot be truly accounted for respite so great is the other tension then.

The bed of the cylinder comprises three distinct zones separated by clear-cut mental or imaginary frontiers invisible to the eye of flesh. First an outer belt roughly one metre wide reserved for the climbers and strange to say favoured by most of the sedentary and vanquished. Next a slightly narrower inner belt where those weary of searching in mid-cylinder slowly revolve in Indian file intent on the periphery. Finally the arena proper representing an area of one hundred and fifty square metres round numbers and chosen hunting ground of the majority. Let numbers be assigned to these three zones and it appears clearly that from the third to the second and inversely the searcher moves at will whereas on entering and leaving the first he is held to a certain discipline. One example among a thousand of the harmony that reigns in the cylinder between order and licence. Thus access to the climbers' reserve is authorized only when one of them leaves it to rejoin the searchers of the arena or exceptionally those of the intermediate zone. While infringement of this rule is rare it does none the less occur as when for example a particularly nervous searcher can no longer resist the lure of the niches and tries to steal in among the climbers without the warrant of a departure. Whereupon he is unfailingly ejected by the queue nearest to the point of trespass and the matter goes no further. No choice then for the searcher wishing to join the climbers but to watch for his opportunity among the searchers of the intermediate zone or searcher-watchers or simply watchers. So much for access to the ladders. In the other direction the passage is not free either and once among the climbers the watcher is there for some time and more precisely the highly variable time it takes to advance from the tail to the head of the queue adopted. For no less than the freedom for each body to climb is the obligation once in the queue of its choice to queue on to the end. Any attempt to leave prematurely is sharply countered by the other members and the offender put back in his place. But once at the very foot of the ladder with between him and it only one more return to the ground the aspirant is free to rejoin the searchers of the arena or exceptionally the watchers of the intermediate zone without opposition. It is therefore on those at the head of their lines as being the most likely to create the vacancy so ardently desired that the eyes of the second-zone watchers are fixed as they burn to enter the first. The objects of this scrutiny continue so up to the moment they exercise their right to the ladder and take it over. For the climber may reach the head of the queue with the firm resolve to ascend and then feel this melt little by little and gather in its stead the urge to depart but still without the power to decide him till the very last moment when his predecessor is actually on the way down and the ladder virtually his at last. To be noted also the possibility for the climber to leave the queue once he has reached the head and yet not leave the zone. This merely requires his joining one of the other fourteen queues at his disposal or more simply still his returning to the tail of his own. But it is exceptional for a body in the first place to leave its queue and in the second having exceptionally done so not to leave the zone. No alternative then once among the climbers but to stay there at least the time it takes to advance from the last place to the first of the chosen queue. This time varies according to the length of the latter and the more or less prolonged occupation of the ladder. Some users keep it till the last moment. For others one half or any other fraction of this time is enough. The short queue is not necessarily the most rapid and such a one starting tenth may well find himself first before such another starting fifth assuming of course they start together. This being so no wonder that the choice of the queue is determined by considerations having nothing to do with its length. Not that all choose nor even the greater number. The tendency would be rather to join straightway the queue nearest to the point of penetration on condition however that this does not involve motion against the stream. For one entering this zone head-on the nearest queue is on the right and if it does not please it is only by going right that a more pleasing can be found. Some could thus revolve through thousands of degrees before settling down to wait were it not for the rule forbidding them to exceed a single circuit. Any attempt to elude it is quelled by the queue nearest to the point of full circle and the culprit compelled to join its ranks since obviously the right to turn back is denied him too. That a full round should be authorized is eloquent of the tolerant spirit which in the cylinder tempers discipline. But whether chosen or first to hand the queue must be suffered to the end before the climber may leave the zone. First chance of departure therefore at any moment between arrival at head of queue and predecessor's return to ground. There remains to clarify in this same context the situation of the body which having accomplished its queue and let pass the first chance of departure and exercised its right to the ladder returns to the ground. It is now free again to depart without further ado but with no compulsion to do so. And to remain among the climbers it has merely to join again in the same conditions as before the queue so lately left with departure again possible from the moment the head is reached. And should it for some reason or another feel like a little change of queue and ladder it is entitled for the purpose of fixing its choice to a further full circuit in the same way as on first arrival and in the same conditions with this slight difference that having already suffered one queue to the end it is free at any moment of the new revolution to leave the zone. And so on infinitely. Whence theoretically the possibility for those already among the climbers never to leave and never to arrive for those not yet. That there exists no regulation tending to forestall such injustice shows clearly it can never be more than temporary. As indeed it cannot. For the passion to search is such that no place may be left unsearched. To the watcher nevertheless on the qui vive for a departure the wait may seem interminable. Sometimes unable to endure it any longer and fortified by the long vacation he renounces the ladder and resumes his search in the arena. So much roughly speaking for the main ground divisions and the duties and prerogatives of the bodies in their passage from one to another. All has not been told and never shall be. What principle of priority obtains among the watchers always in force and eager to profit by the first departure from among the climbers and whose order of arrival on the scene cannot be established by the queue impracticable in their case or by any other means? Is there not reason to fear a saturation of the intermediate zone and what would be its consequences for the bodies as a whole and particularly for those of the arena thus cut off from the ladders? Is not the cylinder doomed in a more or less distant future to a state of anarchy given over to fury and violence? To these questions and many more the answers are clear and easy to give. It only remains to dare. The sedentary call for no special remark since only the ladders can wean them from their fixity. The vanquished are obviously in no way concerned.

The effect of this climate on the soul is not to be underestimated. But it suffers certainly less than the skin whose entire defensive system from sweat to goose bumps is under constant stress. It continues none the less feebly to resist and indeed honourably compared to the eye which with the best will in the world it is difficult not to consign at the close of all its efforts to nothing short of blindness. For skin in its own way as it is not to mention its humours and lids it has not merely one adversary to contend with. The desiccation of the envelope robs nudity of much of its charm as pink turns grey and transforms into a rustling of nettles the natural succulence of flesh against flesh. The mucous membrane itself is affected which would not greatly matter were it not for its hampering effect on the work of love. But even from this point of view no great harm is done so rare is erection in the cylinder. It does occur none the less followed by more or less happy penetration in the nearest tube. Even man and wife may sometimes be seen in virtue of the law of probabilities to come together again in this way without their knowledge. The spectacle then is one to be remembered of frenzies prolonged in pain and hopelessness long beyond what even the most gifted lovers can achieve in camera. For male or female all are acutely aware how rare the occasion is and how unlikely to recur. But here too the desisting and deathly still in attitudes verging at times on the obscene whenever the vibrations cease and for as long as the crisis lasts. Stranger still at such times all the questing eyes that suddenly go still and fix their stare on the void or on some old abomination as for instance other eyes and then the long looks exchanged by those fain to look away. Irregular intervals of such length separate these lulls that for forgetters the likes of these each is the first. Whence invariably the same vivacity of reaction as to the end of a world and the same brief amaze when the twofold storm resumes and they start to search again neither glad nor even sorry.

Seen from below the wall presents an unbroken surface all the way round and up to the ceiling. And yet its upper half is riddled with niches. This paradox is explained by the levelling effect of the dim omnipresent light. None has ever been known to seek out a niche from below. The eyes are seldom raised and when they are it is to the ceiling. Floor and ceiling bear no sign or mark apt to serve as a guide. The feet of the ladders pitched always at the same points leave no trace. The same is true of the skulls and fists dashed against the wall. Even did such marks exist the light would prevent their being seen. The climber making off with his ladder to plant it elsewhere relies largely on feel. He is seldom out by more than a few centimetres and never by more than a metre at most because of the way the niches are disposed. On the spur of his passion his agility is such that even this deviation does not prevent him from gaining the nearest if not the desired niche and thence though with greater labour from regaining the ladder for the descent. There does none the less exist a north in the guise of one of the vanquished or better one of the women vanquished or better still the woman vanquished. She squats against the wall with her head between her knees and her legs in her arms. The left hand clasps the right shinbone and the right the left forearm. The red hair tarnished by the light hangs to the ground. It hides the face and whole front of the body down to the crutch. The left foot is crossed on the right. She is the north. She rather than some other among the vanquished because of her greater fixity. To one bent for once on taking his bearings she may be of help. For the climber averse to avoidable acrobatics a given niche may lie so many paces or metres to east or west of the woman vanquished without of course his naming her thus or otherwise even in his thoughts. It goes without saying that only the vanquished hide their faces though not all without exception. Standing or sitting with head erect some content themselves with opening their eyes no more. It is of course forbidden to withhold the face or other part from the searcher who demands it and may without fear of resistance remove the hand from the flesh it hides or raise the lid to examine the eye. Some searchers there are who join the climbers with no thought of climbing and simply in order to inspect at close hand one or more among the vanquished or sedentary. The hair of the woman vanquished has thus many a time been gathered up and drawn back and the head raised and the face laid bare and whole front of the body down to the crutch. The inspection once completed it is usual to put everything carefully back in place as far as possible. It is enjoined by a certain ethics not to do unto others what coming from them might give offence. This precept is largely observed in the cylinder in so far as it does not jeopardize the quest which would clearly be a mockery if in case of doubt it were not possible to check certain details. Direct action with a view to their elucidation is generally reserved for the persons of the sedentary and vanquished. Face or back to the wall these normally offer but a single aspect and so may have to be turned the other way. But wherever there is motion as in the arena or among the watchers and the possibility of encompassing the object there is no call for such manipulations. There are times of course when a body has to be brought to a stand and disposed in a certain position to permit the inspection at close hand of a particular part or the search for a scar or birthblot for example. To be noted finally the immunity in this respect of those queueing for a ladder. Obliged for want of space to huddle together over long periods they appear to the observer a mere jumble of mingled flesh. Woe the rash searcher who carried away by his passion dare lay a finger on the least among them. Like a single body the whole queue falls on the offender. Of all the scenes of violence the cylinder has to offer none approaches this.

So on infinitely until towards the unthinkable end if this notion is maintained a last body of all by feeble fits and starts is searching still. There is nothing at first sight to distinguish him from the others dead still where they stand or sit in abandonment beyond recall. Lying down is unheard of in the cylinder and this pose solace of the vanquished is for ever denied them here. Such privation is partly to be explained by the dearth of floor space namely a little under one square metre at the disposal of each body and not to be eked out by that of the niches and tunnels reserved for the search alone. Thus the prostration of those withered ones filled with the horror of contact and compelled to brush together without ceasing is denied its natural end. But the persistence of the twofold vibration suggests that in this old abode all is not yet quite for the best. And sure enough there he stirs this last of all if a man and slowly draws himself up and some time later opens his burnt eyes. At the foot of the ladders propped against the wall with scant regard to harmony no climber waits his turn. The aged vanquished of the third zone has none about him now but others in his image motionless and bowed. The mite still in the white-haired woman's clasp is no more than a shadow in her lap. Seen from the front the red head sunk to the uttermost exposes part of the nape. There he opens then his eyes this last of all if a man and some time later threads his way to that first among the vanquished so often taken for a guide. On his knees he parts the heavy hair and raises the unresisting head. Once devoured the face thus laid bare the eyes at a touch of the thumbs open without demur. In those calm wastes he lets his wander till they are the first to close and the head relinquished falls back into its place. He himself after a pause impossible to time finds at last his place and pose whereupon dark descends and at the same instant the temperature comes to rest not far from freezing point. Hushed in the same breath the faint stridulence mentioned above whence suddenly such silence as to drown all the faint breathings put together. So much roughly speaking for the last state of the cylinder and of this little people of searchers one first of whom if a man in some unthinkable past for the first time bowed his head if this notion is maintained.

Ping

All known all white bare white body fixed one yard legs joined like sewn. Light heat white floor one square yard never seen. White walls one yard by two white ceiling one square yard never seen. Bare white body fixed only the eyes only just. Traces blurs light grey almost white on white. Hands hanging palms front white feet heels together right angle. Light heat white planes shining white bare white body fixed ping fixed elsewhere. Traces blurs signs no meaning light grey almost white. Bare white body fixed white on white invisible. Only the eyes only just light blue almost white. Head haught eyes light blue almost white silence within. Brief murmurs only just almost never all known. Traces blurs signs no meaning light grey almost white. Legs joined like sewn heels together right angle. Traces alone unover given black light grey almost white on white. Light heat white walls shining white one yard by two. Bare white body fixed one yard ping fixed elsewhere. Traces blurs signs no meaning light grey almost white. White feet toes joined like sewn heels together right angle invisible. Eyes alone unover given blue light blue almost white. Murmur only just almost never one second perhaps not alone. Given rose only just bare white body fixed one yard white on white invisible. All white all known murmurs only just almost never always the same all known. Light heat hands hanging palms front white on white invisible. Bare white body fixed ping fixed elsewhere. Only the eyes only just light blue almost white fixed front. Ping murmur only just almost never one second perhaps a way out. Head haught eyes light blue almost white fixed front ping murmur ping silence. Eyes holes light blue almost white mouth white seam like sewn invisible. Ping murmur perhaps a nature one second almost never that much memory almost never. White walls each its trace grey blur signs no meaning light grey almost white. Light heat all known all white planes meeting invisible. Ping murmur only just almost never one second perhaps a meaning that much memory almost never. White feet toes joined like sewn heels together right angle ping elsewhere no sound. Hands hanging palms front legs front legs joined like sewn. Head haught eyes holes light blue almost white fixed front silence within. Ping elsewhere always there but that known not. Eyes holes light blue alone unover given blue light blue almost white only colour fixed front. All white all known white planes shining white ping murmur only just almost never one second light time that much memory almost never. Bare white body fixed one yard ping fixed elsewhere white on white invisible heart breath no sound. Only the eyes given blue light blue almost white fixed front only colour alone unover. Planes meeting invisible one only shining white infinite but that known not. Nose ears white holes mouth white seam like sewn invisible. Ping murmurs only just almost never one second always the same all known. Given rose only just bare white body fixed one yard invisible all known without within. Ping perhaps a nature one second with image same time a little less blue and white in the wind. White ceiling shining white one square yard never seen ping perhaps way out there one second ping silence. Traces alone unover given black grey blurs signs no meaning light grey almost white always the same. Ping perhaps not alone one second with image always the same same time a little less that much memory almost never ping silence. Given rose only just nails fallen white over. Long hair fallen white invisible over. White scars invisible same white as flesh torn of old given rose only just. Ping image only just almost never one second light time blue and white in the wind. Head haught nose ears white holes mouth white seam like sewn invisible over. Only the eyes given blue fixed front light blue almost white only colour alone unover. Light heat white planes shining white one only shining white infinite but that known not. Ping a nature only just almost never one second with image same time a little less blue and white in the wind. Traces blurs light grey eyes holes light blue almost white fixed front ping a meaning only just almost never ping silence. Bare white one yard fixed ping fixed elsewhere no sound legs joined like sewn heels together right angle hands hanging palms front. Head haught eyes holes light blue almost white fixed front silence within. Ping elsewhere always there but that known not. Ping perhaps not alone one second with image same time a little less dim eye black and white half closed long lashes imploring that much memory almost never. Afar flash of time all white all over all of old ping flash white walls shining white no trace eyes holes light blue almost white last colour ping white over. Ping fixed last elsewhere legs joined like sewn heels together right angle hands hanging palms front head haught eyes white invisible fixed front over. Given rose only just one yard invisible bare white all known without within over. White ceiling never seen ping of old only just almost never one second light time white floor never seen ping of old perhaps there. Ping of old only just perhaps a meaning a nature one second almost never blue and white in the wind that much memory henceforth never. White planes no trace shining white one only shining white infinite but that known now. Light heat all known all white heart breath no sound. Head haught eyes white fixed front old ping last murmur one second perhaps not alone eye unlustrous black and white half closed long lashes imploring ping silence ping over.

Lessness

Ruins true refuge long last towards which so many false time out of mind. All sides endlessness earth sky as one no sound no stir. Grey face two pale blue little body heart beating only upright. Blacked out fallen open four walls over backwards true refuge issueless.

Scattered ruins same grey as the sand ash grey true refuge. Four square all light sheer white blank planes all gone from mind. Never was but grey air timeless no sound figment the passing light. No sound no stir ash grey sky mirrored earth mirrored sky. Never but this changelessness dream the passing hour.

He will curse God again as in the blessed days face to the open sky the passing deluge. Little body grey face features crack and little holes two pale blue. Blank planes sheer white eye calm long last all gone from mind.

Figment light never was but grey air timeless no sound. Blank planes touch close sheer white all gone from mind. Little body ash grey locked rigid heart beating face to endlessness. On him will rain again as in the blessed days of blue the passing cloud. Four square true refuge long last four walls over backwards no sound.

Grey sky no cloud no sound no stir earth ash grey sand. Little body same grey as the earth sky ruins only upright. Ash grey all sides earth sky as one all sides endlessness.

He will stir in the sand there will be stir in the sky the air the sand. Never but in dream the happy dream only one time to serve. Little body little block heart beating ash grey only upright. Earth sky as one all sides endlessness little body only upright. In the sand no hold one step more in the endlessness he will make it. No sound not a breath same grey all sides earth sky body ruins.

Slow black with ruin true refuge four walls over backwards no sound. Legs a single block arms fast to sides little body face to endlessness. Never but in vanished dream the passing hour long short. Only upright little body grey smooth no relief a few holes. One step in the ruins in the sand on his back in the endlessness he will make it. Never but dream the days and nights made of dreams of other nights better days. He will live again the space of a step it will be day and night again over him the endlessness.

In four split asunder over backwards true refuge issueless scattered ruins. Little body little block genitals overrun arse a single block grey crack overrun. True refuge long last issueless scattered down four walls over backwards no sound. All sides endlessness earth sky as one no stir not a breath. Blank planes sheer white calm eye light of reason all gone from mind. Scattered ruins ash grey all sides true refuge long last issueless.

Ash grey little body only upright heart beating face to end-lessness. Old love new love as in the blessed days unhappiness will reign again. Earth sand same grey as the air sky ruins body fine ash grey sand. Light refuge sheer white blank planes all gone from mind. Flatness endless little body only upright same grey all sides earth sky body ruins. Face to white calm touch close eye calm long last all gone from mind. One step more one alone all alone in the sand no hold he will make it.

Blacked out fallen open true refuge issueless towards which so many false time out of mind. Never but silence such that in imagination this wild laughter these cries. Head through calm eye all light white calm all gone from mind. Figment dawn dispeller of figments and the other called dusk.

He will go on his back face to the sky open again over him the ruins the sand the endlessness. Grey air timeless earth sky as one same grey as the ruins flatness endless. It will be day and night again over him the endlessness the air heart will beat again. True refuge long last scattered ruins same grey as the sand.

Face to calm eye touch close all calm all white all gone from mind. Never but imagined the blue in a wild imagining the blue celeste of poesy. Little void mighty light four square all white blank planes all gone from mind. Never was but grey air timeless no stir not a breath. Heart beating little body only upright grey face features overrun two pale blue. Light white touch close head through calm eye light of reason all gone from mind.

Little body same grey as the earth sky ruins only upright. No sound not a breath same grey all sides earth sky body ruins. Blacked out fallen open four walls over backwards true refuge issueless.

No sound no stir ash grey sky mirrored earth mirrored sky. Grey air timeless earth sky as one same grey as the ruins flatness endless. In the sand no hold one step more in the endlessness he will make it. It will be day and night again over him the endlessness the air heart will beat again.

Figment light never was but grey air timeless no sound. All sides endlessness earth sky as one no stir not a breath. On him will rain again as in the blessed days of blue the passing cloud. Grey sky no cloud no sound no stir earth ash grey sand.

Little void mighty light four square all white blank planes all gone from mind. Flatness endless little body only upright same grey all sides earth sky body ruins. Scattered ruins same grey as the sand ash grey true refuge. Four square true refuge long last four walls over backwards no sound. Never but this change-lessness dream the passing hour. Never was but grey air timeless no sound figment the passing light.

In four split asunder over backwards true refuge issueless scattered ruins. He will live again the space of a step it will be day and night again over him the endlessness. Face to white calm touch close eye calm long last all gone from mind. Grey face two pale blue little body heart beating only upright. He will go on his back face to the sky open again over him the ruins the sand the endlessness. Earth sand same grey as the air sky ruins body fine ash grey sand. Blank planes touch close sheer white all gone from mind.

Heart beating little body only upright grey face features overrun two pale blue. Only upright little body grey smooth no relief a few holes. Never but dream the days and nights made of dreams of other nights better days. He will stir in the sand there will be stir in the sky the air the sand. One step in the ruins in the sand on his back in the endlessness he will make it.

Never but silence such that in imagination this wild laughter these cries.

True refuge long last scattered ruins same grey as the sand. Never was but grey air timeless no stir not a breath. Blank planes sheer white calm eye light of reason all gone from mind. Never but in vanished dream the passing hour long short. Four square all light sheer white blank planes all gone from mind.

Blacked out fallen open true refuge issueless towards which so many false time out of mind. Head through calm eye all light white calm all gone from mind. Old love new love as in the blessed days unhappiness will reign again. Ash grey all sides earth sky as one all sides endlessness. Scattered ruins ash grey all sides true refuge long last issueless. Never but in dream the happy dream only one time to serve. Little body grey face features crack and little holes two pale blue.

Ruins true refuge long last towards which so many false time out of mind. Never but imagined the blue in a wild imagining the blue celeste of poesy. Light white touch close head through calm eye light of reason all gone from mind.

Slow black with ruin true refuge four walls over backwards no sound. Earth sky as one all sides endlessness little body only upright. One step more one alone all alone in the sand no hold he will make it. Ash grey little body only upright heart beating face to endlessness. Light refuge sheer white blank planes all gone from mind. All sides endlessness earth sky as one no sound no stir.

Legs a single block arms fast to sides little body face to endlessness. True refuge long last issueless scattered down four walls over backwards no sound. Blank planes sheer white eye calm long last all gone from mind. He will curse God again as in the blessed days face to the open sky the passing deluge. Face to calm eye touch close all calm all white all gone from mind.

Little body little block heart beating ash grey only upright. Little body ash grey locked rigid heart beating face to endlessness. Little body little block genitals overrun arse a single block grey crack overrun. Figment dawn dispeller of figments and the other called dusk.

Fizzles

He is barehead

He is barehead, barefoot, clothed in a singlet and tight trousers too short for him, his hands have told him so, again and again, and his feet, feeling each other and rubbing against the legs, up and down calves and shins. To this vaguely prison garb none of his memories answer, so far, but all are of heaviness, in this connexion, of fullness and of thickness. The great head where he toils is all mockery, he is forth again, he'll be back again. Some day he'll see himself, his whole front, from the chest down, and the arms, and finally the hands, first rigid at arm's length, then close up, trembling, to his eyes. He halts, for the first time since he knows he's under way, one foot before the other, the higher flat, the lower on its toes, and waits for a decision. Then he moves on. Spite of the dark he does not grope his way, arms outstretched, hands agape and the feet held back just before the ground. With the result he must often, namely at every turn, strike against the walls that hem his path, against the right-hand when he turns left, the left-hand when he turns right, now with this foot, now with the crown of his head, for he holds himself bowed, because of the rise, and because he always holds himself bowed, his back humped, his head thrust forward, his eyes cast down. He loses his blood, but in no great quantity, the little wounds have time to close before being opened again, his pace is so slow. There are places where the walls almost meet, then it is the shoulders take the shock. But instead of stopping short, and even turning back, saying to himself, This is the end of the road, nothing now but to return to the other terminus and start again, instead he attacks the narrow sideways and so finally squeezes through, to the great hurt of his chest and back. Do his eyes, after such long exposure to the gloom, begin to pierce it? No, and this is one of the reasons why he shuts them more and more, more and more often and for ever longer spells. For his concern is increasingly to spare himself needless fatigue, such as that come of staring before him, and even all about him, hour after hour, day after day, and never seeing a thing. This is not the time to go into his wrongs, but perhaps he was wrong not to persist, in his efforts to pierce the gloom. For he might well have succeeded, in the end, up to a point, which would have brightened things up for him, nothing like a ray of light, from time to time, to brighten things up for one. And all may yet grow light, at any moment, first dimly and then – how can one say? – then more and more, till all is flooded with light, the way, the ground, the walls, the vault, without his being one whit the wiser. The moon may appear, framed at the end of the vista, and he in no state to rejoice and quicken his step, or on the contrary wheel and run, while there is yet time. For the moment however no complaints, which is the main. The legs notably seem in good shape, that is a blessing, Murphy had first-rate legs. The head is still a little weak, it needs time to get going again, that part does. No sign of insanity in any case, that is a blessing. Meagre equipment, but well balanced. The heart? No complaints. It's going again, enough to see him through. But see how now, having turned right for example, instead of turning left a little further on he turns right again. And see how now again, yet a little further on, instead of turning left at last he turns right yet again. And so on until, instead of turning right yet again, as he expected, he turns left at last. Then for a time his zigzags resume their tenor, deflecting him alternately to right and left, that is to say bearing him onward in a straight line more or less, but no longer the same straight line as when he set forth, or rather as when he suddenly realized he was forth, or perhaps after all the same. For if there are long periods when the right predominates, there are others when the left prevails. It matters little in any case, so long as he keeps on climbing. But see how now a little further on the ground falls away so sheer that he has to rear violently backward in order not to fall. Where is it then that life awaits him, in relation to his starting-point, to the point rather at which he suddenly realized he was started, above or below? Or

will they cancel out in the end, the long gentle climbs and headlong steeps? It matters little in any case, so long as he is on the
right road, and that he is, for there are no others, unless he has
let them slip by unnoticed, one after another. Walls and ground,
if not of stone, are no less hard, to the touch, and wet. The
former, certain days, he stops to lick. The fauna, if any, is silent.
The only sounds, apart from those of the body on its way, are of
fall, a great drop dropping at last from a great height and bursting, a solid mass that leaves its place and crashes down, lighter
particles collapsing slowly. Then the echo is heard, as loud at
first as the sound that woke it and repeated sometimes a good
score of times, each time a little weaker, no, sometimes louder
than the time before, till finally it dies away. Then silence again,
broken only by the sound, intricate and faint, of the body on its
way. But such sounds of fall are not common and mostly silence
reigns, broken only by the sounds of the body on its way, of the
bare feet on the wet ground, of the laboured breathing, of the
body striking against the walls or squeezing through the nar-
rows, of the clothes, singlet and trousers, espousing and resisting
the movements of the body, coming unstuck from the damp
flesh and sticking to it again, tattering and fluttered where in
tatters already by sudden flurries as suddenly stilled, and finally
of the hands as now and then they pass, back and forth, over
all those parts of the body they can reach without fatigue. He
himself has yet to drop. The air is foul. Sometimes he halts and
leans against a wall, his feet wedged against the other. He has
already a number of memories, from the memory of the day he
suddenly knew he was there, on this same path still bearing him
along, to that now of having halted to lean against the wall, he
has a little past already, even a smatter of settled ways. But it is
all still fragile. And often he surprises himself, both moving and
at rest, but more often moving, for he seldom comes to rest, as
destitute of history as on that first day, on this same path, which
is his beginning, on days of great recall. But usually now, the
surprise once past, memory returns and takes him back, if he
will, far back to that first instant beyond which nothing, when he

was already old, that is to say near to death, and knew, though unable to recall having lived, what age and death are, with other momentous matters. But it is all still fragile. And often he suddenly begins, in these black windings, and makes his first steps for quite a while before realizing they are merely the last, or latest. The air is so foul that only he seems fitted to survive it who never breathed the other, the true life-giving, or so long ago as to amount to never. And such true air, coming hard on that of here, would very likely prove fatal, after a few lungfuls. But the change from one to the other will no doubt be gentle, when the time comes, and gradual, as the man draws closer and closer to the open. And perhaps even now the air is less foul than when he started, than when he suddenly realized he was started. In any case little by little his history takes shape, with if not yet exactly its good days and bad, at least studded with occasions passing rightly or wrongly for outstanding, such as the straitest narrow, the loudest fall, the most lingering collapse, the steepest descent, the greatest number of successive turns the same way, the greatest fatigue, the longest rest, the longest – aside from the sound of the body on its way – silence. Ah yes, and the most rewarding passage of the hands, on the one hand, the feet, on the other, over all those parts of the body within their reach. And the sweetest wall lick. In a word all the summits. Then other summits, hardly less elevated, such as a shock so rude that it rivalled the rudest of all. Then others still, scarcely less eminent, a wall lick so sweet as to vie with the second sweetest. Then little or nothing of note till the minima, these too unforgettable, on days of great recall, a sound of fall so muted by the distance, or for want of weight, or for lack of space between departure and arrival, that it was perhaps his fancy. Or again, second example, no, not a good example. Other landmarks still are provided by first times, and even second. Thus the first narrow, for example, no doubt because he was not expecting it, impressed him quite as strongly as the straitest, just as the second collapse, no doubt because he was expecting it, was no less than the briefest never to be forgotten. So with one thing and another little by little his

138

history takes shape, and even changes shape, as new maxima and minima tend to cast into the shade, and toward oblivion, those momentarily glorified, and as fresh elements and motifs, such as these bones of which more very shortly, and at length, in view of their importance, contribute to enrich it.

Horn came always

Horn came always at night. I received him in the dark. I had
come to bear everything bar being seen. In the beginning I
would send him away after five or six minutes. Till he learnt to
go of his own accord, once his time was up. He consulted his
notes by the light of an electric torch. Then he switched it off
and spoke in the dark. Light silence, dark speech. It was five or
six years since anyone had seen me, to begin with myself. I mean
the face I had pored over so, all down the years. Now I would
resume that inspection, that it may be a lesson to me, in my
mirrors and looking-glasses so long put away. I'll let myself be
seen before I'm done. I'll call out, if there is a knock, Come in!
But I speak now of five or six years ago. These allusions to now,
to before and after, and all such yet to come, that we may feel
ourselves in time. I had more trouble with the body proper. I
masked it as best I could, but when I got out of bed it was sure
to show. For I was now beginning, then if you prefer, to get out
of bed again. Then there is the matter of its injuries. But the
body was of less consequence. Whereas the face, no, not at any
price. Hence Horn at night. When he forgot his torch he made
shift with matches. Were I to ask, for example, And her gown
that day?, then he switched on, thumbed through his notes,
found the particular, switched off and answered, for example,
The yellow. He did not like one to interrupt him and I must
confess I seldom had call to. Interrupting him one night I asked
him to light his face. He did so, briefly, switched off and
resumed the thread. Interrupting again I asked him to be silent
for a moment. That night things went no further. But the next,
or more likely the next but one, I desired him at the outset to
light his face and keep it lit till further notice. The light, bright at
first, gradually died down to no more than a yellow glimmer
which then, to my surprise, persisted undiminished some little

while. Then suddenly it was dark again and Horn went away, the five or six minutes having presumably expired. But here one of two things, either the final extinction had coincided, by some prank of chance, with the close of the session, or else Horn, knowing his time to be up, had cut off the last dribs of current. I still see, sometimes, that waning face disclosing, more and more clearly the more it entered shadow, the one I remembered. In the end I said to myself, as unaccountably it lingered on, No doubt about it, it is he. It is in outer space, not to be confused with the other, that such images develop. I need only interpose my hand, or close my eyes, to banish them, or take off my eyeglasses for them to fade. This is a help, but not a real protection, as we shall see. I try to keep before me therefore, as far as possible, when I get up, some such unbroken plane as that which I command from my bed, I mean the ceiling. For I have taken to getting up again. I thought I had made my last journey, the one I must now try once more to elucidate, that it may be a lesson to me, the one from which it were better I had never returned. But the feeling gains on me that I must undertake another. So I have taken to getting up again and making a few steps in the room, holding on to the bars of the bed. What ruined me at bottom was athletics. With all that jumping and running when I was young, and even long after in the case of certain events, I wore out the machine before its time. My fortieth year had come and gone and I still throwing the javelin.

Afar a bird

Ruinstrewn land, he has trodden it all night long, I gave up, hugging the hedges, between road and ditch, on the scant grass, little slow steps, no sound, stopping ever and again, every ten steps say, little wary steps, to catch his breath, then listen, ruinstrewn land, I gave up before birth, it is not possible otherwise, but birth there had to be, it was he, I was inside, now he stops again, for the hundredth time that night say, that gives the distance gone, it's the last, hunched over his stick, I'm inside, it was he who wailed, he who saw the light, I didn't wail, I didn't see the light, one on top of the other the hands weigh on the stick, the head weighs on the hands, he has caught his breath, he can listen now, the trunk horizontal, the legs asprawl, sagging at the knees, same old coat, the stiffened tails stick up behind, day dawns, he has only to raise his eyes, open his eyes, raise his eyes, he merges in the hedge, afar a bird, a moment past he grasps and is fled, it was he had a life, I didn't have a life, a life not worth having, because of me, it's impossible I should have a mind and I have one, someone divines me, divines us, that's what he's come to, come to in the end, I see him in my mind, there divining us, hands and head a little heap, the hours pass, he is still, he seeks a voice for me, it's impossible I should have a voice and I have none, he'll find one for me, ill beseeming me, it will meet the need, his need, but no more of him, that image, the little heap of hands and head, the trunk horizontal, the jutting elbows, the eyes closed and the face rigid listening, the eyes hidden and the whole face hidden, that image and no more, never changing, ruinstrewn land, night recedes, he is fled, I'm inside, he'll do himself to death, because of me, I'll live it with him, I'll live his death, the end of his life and then his death, step by step, in the present, how he'll go about it, it's impossible I should know, I'll know, step by step, it's he will die, I won't die,

143

there will be nothing of him left but bones, I'll be inside, nothing but a little grit, I'll be inside, it is not possible otherwise, ruinstrewn land, he is fled through the hedge, no more stopping now, he will never say I, because of me, he won't speak to anyone, no one will speak to him, he won't speak to himself, there is nothing left in his head, I'll feed it all it needs, all it needs to end, to say I no more, to open its mouth no more, confusion of memory and lament, of loved ones and impossible youth, clutching the stick in the middle he stumbles bowed over the fields, a life of my own I tried, in vain, never any but his, worth nothing, because of me, he said it wasn't one, it was, still is, the same, I'm still inside, the same, I'll put faces in his head, names, places, churn them all up together, all he needs to end, phantoms to flee, last phantoms, to flee and to pursue, he'll confuse his mother with whores, his father with a roadman named Balfe, I'll feed him an old curdog, a mangy old curdog, that he may love again, lose again, ruinstrewn land, little panic steps

I gave up before birth

I gave up before birth, it is not possible otherwise, but birth there had to be, it was he, I was inside, that's how I see it, it was he who wailed, he who saw the light, I didn't wail, I didn't see the light, it's impossible I should have a voice, impossible I should have thoughts, and I speak and think, I do the impossible, it is not possible otherwise, it was he who had a life, I didn't have a life, a life not worth having, because of me, he'll do himself to death, because of me, I'll tell the tale, the tale of his death, the end of his life and his death, his death alone would not be enough, not enough for me, if he rattles it's he who will rattle, I won't rattle, he who will die, I won't die, perhaps they will bury him, if they find him, I'll be inside, he'll rot, I won't rot, there will be nothing of him left but bones, I'll be inside, nothing left but dust, I'll be inside, it is not possible otherwise, that's how I see it, the end of his life and his death, how he will go about it, go about coming to an end, it's impossible I should know, I'll know, step by step, impossible I should tell, I'll tell, in the present, there will be no more talk of me, only of him, of the end of his life and his death, of his burial if they find him, that will be the end, I won't go on about worms, about bones and dust, no one cares about them, unless I'm bored in his dust, that would surprise me, as stiff as I was in his flesh, here long silence, perhaps he'll drown, he always wanted to drown, he didn't want them to find him, he can't want now any more, but he used to want to drown, he usen't to want them to find him, deep water and a millstone, urge spent like all the others, but why one day to the left, to the left and not elsewhither, here long silence, there will be no more I, he'll never say I any more, he'll never say anything any more, he won't talk to anyone, no one will talk to him, he won't talk to himself, he won't think any more, he'll go on, I'll be inside, he'll come to a place and drop, why there and

145

not elsewhere, drop and sleep, badly because of me, he'll get up and go on, badly because of me, he can't stay still any more, because of me, he can't go on any more, because of me, there's nothing left in his head, I'll feed it all it needs.

Closed place

Closed place. All needed to be known for say is known. There is nothing but what is said. Beyond what is said there is nothing. What goes on in the arena is not said. Did it need to be known it would be. No interest. Not for imagining. Place consisting of an arena and a ditch. Between the two skirting the latter a track. Closed place. Beyond the ditch there is nothing. This is known because it needs to be said. Arena black vast. Room for millions. Wandering and still. Never seeing never hearing one another. Never touching. No more is known. Depth of ditch. See from the edge all the bodies on its bed. The millions still there. They appear six times smaller than life. Bed divided into lots. Dark and bright. They take up all its width. The lots still bright are square. Appear square. Just room for the average sized body. Stretched out diagonally. Bigger it has to curl up. Thus the width of the ditch is known. It would have been in any case. Sum the bright lots. The dark. Outnumbered the former by far. The place is already old. The ditch is old. In the beginning it was all bright. All bright lots. Almost touching. Faintly edged with shadow. The ditch seems straight. Then reappears a body seen before. A closed curve therefore. Brilliance of the bright lots. It does not encroach on the dark. Adamantine blackness of these. As dense at the edge as at the centre. But vertically it diffuses unimpeded. High above the level of the arena. As high above as the ditch is deep. In the black air towers of pale light. So many bright lots so many towers. So many bodies visible on the bed. The track follows the ditch all the way along. All the way round. It is on a higher level than the arena. A step higher. It is made of dead leaves. A reminder of beldam nature. They are dry. The heat and the dry air. Dead but not rotting. Crumbling into dust rather. Just wide enough for one. On it no two ever meet.

Old earth

Old earth, no more lies, I've seen you, it was me, with my other's ravening eyes, too late. You'll be on me, it will be you, it will be me, it will be us, it was never us. It won't be long now, perhaps not tomorrow, nor the day after, but too late. Not long now, how I gaze on you, and what refusal, how you refuse me, you so refused. It's a cockchafer year, next year there won't be any, nor the year after, gaze your fill. I come home at nightfall, they take to wing, rise from my little oaktree and whirr away, glutted, into the shadows. I reach up, grasp the bough, pull myself up and go in. Three years in the earth, those the moles don't get, then guzzle guzzle, ten days long, a fortnight, and always the flight at nightfall. To the river perhaps, they head for the river. I turn on the light, then off, ashamed, stand at gaze before the window, the windows, going from one to another, leaning on the furniture. For an instant I see the sky, the different skies, then they turn to faces, agonies, loves, the different loves, happiness too, yes, there was that too, unhappily. Moments of life, of mine too, among others, no denying, all said and done. Happiness, what happiness, but what deaths, what loves, I knew at the time, it was too late then. Ah to love at your last and see them at theirs, the last minute loved ones, and be happy, why ah, uncalled for. No but now, now, simply stay still, standing before a window, one hand on the wall, the other clutching your shirt, and see the sky, a long gaze, but no, gasps and spasms, a childhood sea, other skies, another body.

For to end yet again

For to end yet again skull alone in a dark place pent bowed on
a board to begin. Long thus to begin till the place fades followed
by the board long after. For to end yet again skull alone in the dark
the void no neck no face just the box last place of all in the
dark the void. Place of remains where once used to gleam in the
dark on and off used to glimmer a remain. Remains of the days
of the light of day never light so faint as theirs so pale. Thus then
the skull makes to glimmer again in lieu of going out. There in the
end all at once or by degrees there dawns and magic lingers a
leaden dawn. By degrees less dark till final grey or all at once as if
switched on grey sand as far as eye can see beneath grey cloudless
sky same grey. Skull last place of all black void within without till
all at once or by degrees this leaden dawn at last checked no
sooner dawned. Grey cloudless sky grey sand as far as eye can see
long desert to begin. Sand pale as dust ah but dust indeed deep to
engulf the haughtiest monuments which too it once was here and
there. There in the end same grey invisible to any other eye stark
erect amidst his ruins the expelled. Same grey all that little body
from head to feet sunk ankle deep were it not for the eyes last
bright of all. The arms still cleave to the trunk and to each other
the legs made for flight. Grey cloudless sky ocean of dust not a
ripple mock confines verge upon verge hell air not a breath.
Mingling with the dust slowly sinking some almost fully sunk the
ruins of the refuge. First change of all in the end a fragment comes
away and falls. With slow fall for so dense a body it lights like cork
on water and scarce breaks the surface. Thus then the skull last
place of all makes to glimmer again in lieu of going out. Grey
cloudless sky verge upon verge grey timeless air of those nor for
God nor for his enemies. There again in the end way amidst the
verges a light in the grey two white dwarfs. Long at first mere
whiteness from afar they toil step by step through the grey dust

linked by a litter same white seen from above in the grey air. Slowly it sweeps the dust so bowed the backs and long the arms compared with the legs and deep sunk the feet. Bleached as one same wilderness they are so alike the eye cannot tell them apart. They carry face to face and relay each other often so that turn about they backward lead the way. His who follows who knows to shape the course much as the coxswain with light touch the skiff. Let him veer to the north or other cardinal point and promptly the other by as much to the antipode. Let one stop short and the other about this pivot slew the litter through a semi-circle and thereon the roles are reversed. Bone white of the sheet seen from above and the shafts fore and aft and the dwarfs to the crowns of their massy skulls. From time to time impelled as one they let fall the litter then again as one take it up again without having to stoop. It is the dung litter of laughable memory with shafts twice as long as the couch. Swelling the sheet now fore now aft as permutations list a pillow marks the place of the head. At the end of the arms the four hands open as one and the litter so close to the dust already settles without a sound. Monstrous extremities including skulls stunted legs and trunks monstrous arms stunted faces. In the end the feet as one lift clear the left forward backward the right and the amble resumes. Grey dust as far as eye can see beneath grey cloudless sky and there all at once or by degrees this whiteness to decipher. Yet to imagine if he can see it the last expelled amidst his ruins if he can ever see it and seeing believe his eyes. Between him and it bird's-eye view the space grows no less but has only even now appeared last desert to be crossed. Little body last stage of all stark erect still amidst his ruins all silent and marble still. First change of all a fragment comes away from mother ruin and with slow fall scarce stirs the dust. Dust having engulfed so much it can engulf no more and woe the little on the surface still. Or mere digestive torpor as once the boas which past with one last gulp clean sweep at last. Dwarfs distant whiteness sprung from nowhere motionless afar in the grey air where dust alone possible. Wilderness and carriage immemorial as one they advance as one retreat hither thither halt move on again. He facing forward will sometimes halt and hoist as best he can his head as if to scan the void and who knows alter course. Then on so soft the eye does not see them go driftless with heads sunk and lidded eyes. Long lifted to the horizontal faces closer and closer strain as it will the eye achieves no more than two tiny oval blanks. Atop the cyclopean dome rising sheer from jut of brow yearns white to the grey sky the bump of habitativity or love of home. Last change of all in the end the expelled falls headlong down and lies back to sky full little stretch amidst his ruins. Feet centre body radius falls unbending as a statue falls faster and faster the space of a quadrant. Eagle the eye that shall discern him now mingled with the ruins mingling with the dust beneath a sky forsaken of its scavengers. Breath has not left him though soundless still and exhaling scarce ruffles the dust. Eyes in their orbits blue still unlike the doll's the fall has not shut nor yet the dust stopped up. No fear henceforth of his ever having not to believe them before that whiteness afar where sky and dust merge. Whiteness neither on earth nor above of the dwarfs as if at the end of their trials the litter left lying between them the white bodies marble still. Ruins all silent marble still little body prostrate at attention wash blue deep in gaping sockets. As in the days erect the arms still cleave to the trunk and to each other the legs made for flight. Fallen unbending all his little length as though pushed from behind by some helping hand or by the wind but not a breath. Or murmur from some dreg of life after the lifelong stand fall fall never fear no fear of your rising again. Sepulchral skull is this then its last state all set for always litter and dwarfs ruins and little body grey cloud-less sky glutted dust verge upon verge hell air not a breath? And dream of a way in a space with neither here nor there where all the footsteps ever fell can never fare nearer to anywhere nor from any-where further away? No for in the end for to end yet again by degrees or as though switched on dark falls there again that cer-tain dark that alone certain ashes can. Through it who knows yet another end beneath a cloudless sky same dark it earth and sky of a last end if ever there had to be another absolutely had to be.

Still

Bright at last close of a dark day the sun shines out at last and goes down. Sitting quite still at valley window normally turn head now and see it the sun low in the southwest sinking. Even get up certain moods and go stand by western window quite still watching it sink and then the afterglow. Always quite still some reason some time past this hour at open window facing south in small upright wicker chair with armrests. Eyes stare out unseeing till first movement some time past close though unseeing still while still light. Quite still again then all quite quiet apparently till eyes open again while still light though less. Normally turn head now ninety degrees to watch sun which if already gone then fading afterglow. Even get up certain moods and go stand by western window till quite dark and even some evenings some reason long after. Eyes then open again while still light and close again in what if not quite a single movement almost. Quite still again then at open window facing south over the valley in this wicker chair though actually close inspection not still at all but trembling all over. Close inspection namely detail by detail all over to add up finally to this whole not still at all but trembling all over. But casually in this failing light impression dead still even the hands clearly trembling and the breast faint rise and fall. Legs side by side broken right angles at the knees as in that old statue some old god twanged at sunrise and again at sunset. Trunk likewise dead plumb right up to top of skull seen from behind including nape clear of chairback. Arms likewise broken right angles at the elbows forearms along armrests just right length forearms and rests for hands clenched lightly to rest on ends. So quite still again then all quite quiet apparently eyes closed which to anticipate when they open again if they do in time then dark or some degree of starlight or moonlight or both. Normally watch night fall however long from this narrow chair or standing by western window quite still either case. Quite still namely staring at some one thing alone such as tree or bush a detail alone if near if far the whole if far enough till it goes. Or by eastern window certain moods staring at some point on the hillside such as that beech in whose shade once quite still till it goes. Chair some reason always same place same position facing south as though clamped down whereas in reality no lighter no more movable imaginable. Or anywhere any ope staring out at nothing just failing light quite still till quite dark though of course no such thing just less light still when less did not seem possible. Quite still then all this time eyes open when discovered then closed then opened and closed again no other movement any kind though of course not still at all when suddenly or so it looks this movement impossible to follow let alone describe. The right hand slowly opening leaves the armrest taking with it the whole forearm complete with elbow and slowly rises opening further as it goes and turning a little deasil till midway to the head it hesitates and hangs half open trembling in mid air. Hangs there as if half inclined to return that is sink back slowly closing as it goes and turning the other way till as and where it began clenched lightly on end of rest. Here because of what comes now not midway to the head but almost there before it hesitates and hangs there trembling as if half inclined etc. Half no but on the verge when in its turn the head moves from its place forward and down among the ready fingers where no sooner received and held it weighs on down till elbow meeting armrest brings this last movement to an end and all still once more. Here back a little way to that suspense before head to rescue as if hand's need the greater and on down in what if not quite a single movement almost till elbow against rest. All quite still again then head in hand namely thumb on outer edge of right socket index ditto left and middle on left cheekbone plus as the hours pass lesser contacts each more or less now more now less with the faint stirrings of the various parts as night wears on. As if even in the dark eyes closed not enough and perhaps even more than ever necessary against that no such thing the further shelter of the hand. Leave it so all quite still or try listening to the sounds all quite still head in hand listening for a sound.

156

As the Story Was Told

As the story was told me I never went near the place during sessions. I asked what place and a tent was described at length, a small tent the colour of its surroundings. Wearying of this description I asked what sessions and these in their turn were described, their object, duration, frequency and harrowing nature. I hope I was not more sensitive than the next man, but finally I had to raise my hand. I lay there quite still for a time, then asked where I was while all this was going forward. In a hut, was the answer, a small hut in a grove some two hundred yards away, a distance even the loudest cry could not carry, but must die on the way. This was not so strange as at first sight it sounded when one considered the stoutness of the canvas and the sheltered situation of the hut among the trees. Indeed the tent might have been struck where it stood and moved forward fifty yards or so without inconvenience. Lying there with closed eyes in the silence which followed this information I began to see the hut, though unlike the tent it had not been described to me, but only its situation. It reminded me strongly of a summer-house in which as a child I used to sit quite still for hours on end, on the window-seat, the whole year round. It had the same five log walls, the same coloured glass, the same diminutiveness, being not more than ten feet across and so low of ceiling that the average man could not have held himself erect in it, though of course there was no such difficulty for the child. At the centre, facing the coloured panes, stood a small upright wicker chair with arm-rests, as against the summer-house's window-seat. I sat there very straight and still, with my arms along the rests, looking out at the orange light. It must have been shortly after six, the sessions closing punctually at that hour, for as I watched a hand appeared in the doorway and held out to me a sheet of writing. I took and read it, then tore it in four and put the pieces in the

159

waiting hand to take away. A little later the whole scene disappeared. As the story was told me the man succumbed in the end to his ill-treatment, though quite old enough at the time to die naturally of old age. I lay there a long time quite still – even as a child I was unusually still and more and more so with the passing years – till it must have seemed the story was over. But finally I asked if I knew exactly what the man – I would like to give his name but cannot – what exactly was required of the man, what it was he would not or could not say. No, was the answer, after some little hesitation no, I did not know what the poor man was required to say, in order to be pardoned, but would have recognized it at once, yes, at a glance, if I had seen it.

La Falaise/The Cliff

La Falaise

Fenêtre entre ciel et terre on ne sait où. Elle donne sur une falaise incolore. La crête échappe à l'œil où qu'il se mette. La base aussi. Deux pans de ciel à jamais blanc la bordent. Le ciel laisse-t-il deviner une fin de terre? L'éther intermédiaire? D'oiseau de mer pas trace. Ou trop claire pour paraître. Enfin quelle preuve d'une face? L'œil n'en trouve aucune où qu'il se mette. Il se désiste et la folle s'y met. Emerge enfin d'abord l'ombre d'une corniche. Patience elle s'animera de restes mortels. Un crâne entier se dégage pour finir. Un seul d'entre ceux que valent de tels débris. Du coronal il tente encore de rentrer dans la roche. Les orbites laissent entrevoir l'ancien regard. Par instants la falaise disparaît. Alors l'œil de voler vers les blancs lointains. Ou de se détourner de devant.

The Cliff

Window between sky and earth nowhere known. Opening on a colourless cliff. The crest escapes the eye wherever set. The base as well. Framed by two sections of sky forever white. Any hint in the sky at a land's end? The yonder ether? Of sea birds no trace. Or too pale to show. And then what proof of a face? None that the eye can find wherever set. It gives up and the bedlam head takes over. At long last first looms the shadow of a ledge. Patience it will be enlivened with mortal remains. A whole skull emerges in the end. One alone from amongst those such residua evince. Still attempting to sink back its coronal into the rock. The old stare half showing within the orbits. At times the cliff vanishes. Then off the eye flies to the whiteness verge upon verge. Or thence away from it all.

Translated by Edith Fournier

neither

to and fro in shadow from inner to outershadow

from impenetrable self to impenetrable unself by way of neither

as between two lit refuges whose doors once neared gently close,
once turned away from gently part again

beckoned back and forth and turned away

heedless of the way, intent on the one gleam or the other

unheard footfalls only sound

till at last halt for good, absent for good from self and other

then no sound

then gently light unfading on that unheeded neither

unspeakable home

Appendix 1: 'Still' Texts

Sounds

Sounds then even stillest night here where none come some time past mostly no want no not no want but never none of any kind even stillest night seldom an hour another hour but some sound of some kind here where none come none pass even the nightbirds some time past in such numbers once such numbers. Or if none hour after hour no sound of any kind then he having been dreamt away let himself be dreamt away to where none at any time away from here where none come none pass to where no sound at any time no sound to listen for none of any kind. But mostly not for nothing never quite for nothing even stillest night when air too still for even the lightest leaf to sound no not to sound to carry too still for even the lightest leaf to carry the brief way here and not die the sound not die on the brief way the wave not die away. For catch up the torch and out up the path all overgrown now as more than once he must up suddenly out of the chair and out up the path by the torchlight and still no sound from the tree till nearly there when switch out and stand beneath or with his arms round it certain moods and head against the bark as if a human. Then back when enough some nights only after hours switch on and back in silence no sooner in the clear open back down the path by the torchlight as before and no sound but worse than none his feet among the weeds till back in the chair quite still as before. For clearly worse than none the self's when the whole body moves from its place as to those leaves then or some part or parts leaving the main unmoved or even at its most still as now all outwardly at rest head in hand listening trying listening for a sound. Head in hand as shown from when hand rose from rest to new pose at rest on elbow all silent the whole change so worse than none the self's as silent as if none save one faint at the end the faint creak as it gave the wicker made. Start up now snatching up the torch and out up the path no question some time past even stillest night but rather no sound hour after hour or be dreamt away better still dreamt away where no sound to listen for no more than ghosts make or motes in the sun. Room too quite still some time past and loft where such sounds once all night there by open window eyes closed or looking out never an hour but suddenly some sound room or loft low and brief never twice quite the same to wonder over a moment no longer now. Even the wind some time past so often once so loud certain nights he could pace to and fro and no more sound than a ghost or mutter old words once got by heart the very wind as though no more air to move no more than in a void. Breath itself sigh it all out through the mouth that sound then fill again hold and out again so often once sigh upon sigh no question now some time past but quiet as when even the mother can't hear stooped over the crib but has to feel pulse or heart. Leave it so then this stillest night till now of all quite still head in hand as shown listening trying listening for a sound or dreamt away try dreamt away where no such thing no more than ghosts make nothing to listen for no such thing as a sound.

Still 3

Whence when back no knowing where no telling where been how long how it was. Back in the chair at the window before the window head in hand as shown dead still listening again in vain. No not yet not listening again in vain quite yet while the dim questions fade where been how long how it was. For head in hand eyes closed as shown always the same dark now from now all hours of day and night. No nightbird to mean night at least or day at least so faint perhaps mere fancy with the right valley wind the incarnation bell. Or Mother Calvet with the dawn pushing the old go-cart for whatever she might find and back at dusk. Back then and nothing to tell but some soundless place and in the head in the hand where such questions once like ghosts where what how long weirdest of all. Till in imagination from the dead faces faces on off in the dark sudden whites long short then black long short then another so on or the same. White stills all front no expression eyes wide unseeing mouth no expression male female all ages one by one never more at a time. There somewhere some time hers or his or some other creature's try dreamt away saying dreamt away where face after face till hers in the end or his or that other creature's. Where faces in the dark as shown for one in the end even though only once only for a second say back try saying back from there head in hand as shown. For one or more why while at it one alone no one alone one by one none it till perhaps some time in the end that one or none. Size as seen in the life at say arm's length sudden white black all about no known expression eyes its at last not looking lids the ones no expression marble still so long then out.

Appendix 2: Publication History

The following bibliography gives first publication details for all texts presented in this volume, together with their first printing in individual editions or collections. A list of collections of Beckett's shorter prose follows. Publication for Calder is London, Grove Press is New York and for Les Éditions de Minuit, Paris.

Textes pour rien

'Texte pour rien V', *Deucalion* (October 1952)

'Textes pour rien III, VI and X', *Les Lettres Nouvelles* 1 : 3 (May 1953), pp. 267–77

'Texte pour rien XI', *Arts-Spectacles* 418 (3–9 July 1953), p. 5

'Texte pour rien XIII', *Le Disque Vert* 1 : 4 (November–December 1953), pp. 3–5

'Textes pour rien I and XII', *Monde Nouveau/Paru* 10 : 89/90 (May–June 1955), pp. 144–9

Nouvelles et Textes pour rien (Les Éditions de Minuit, 1955)

Texts for Nothing

'Text for Nothing I', *Evergreen Review* 3 : 9 (Summer 1959), pp. 21–4

'Text for Nothing III', *Great French Short Stories*, ed. Germaine Brée (New York: Dell, 1960) [translated by Samuel Beckett and Anthony Bonner]

'Texts for Nothing XII', *Transatlantic Review* 24 (Spring 1967), pp. 15–16

'Text for Nothing VI', *London Magazine* n.s. 7 : 5 (August 1967), pp. 47–50

No's Knife: Collected Shorter Prose 1945–1966 (Calder, 1967; repr. 1975)

Stories and Texts for Nothing (Grove Press, 1967)
Texts for Nothing (Signature Series: Signature 21) (Calder and Boyars, 1974).

From an Abandoned Work
  Trinity News: A Dublin University Weekly 3:17 (7 June 1956), p. 4
  Evergreen Review I:3 (1957), pp. 83–91
  From an Abandoned Work (Faber and Faber, 1958)
  First Love and Other Shorts (Grove Press, 1974)

D'un ouvrage abandonné [translated by Ludovic and Agnes Janvier in collaboration with Beckett]
  D'un ouvrage abandonné (Les Éditions de Minuit, 1967)

Faux Départs
  Kursbuch I (June 1965), pp. 1–5

All Strange Away
  All Strange Away, with illustrations by Edward Gorey (New York: Gotham Book Mart, 1976)
  Journal of Beckett Studies 3 (Summer 1978), pp. 1–9
  All Strange Away (John Calder Ltd, 1979)
  Rockaby and Other Short Pieces (Grove Press, 1981)

Imagination morte imaginez
  Les Lettres nouvelles 13 (October–November 1965), pp. 13–16
  Imagination morte imaginez (Les Éditions de Minuit, 1965)

Imagination Dead Imagine
  Sunday Times (7 November 1965), p. 48
  Imagination Dead Imagine (John Calder Ltd, 1965) [trade edition 1966]
  Evergreen Review 10:39 (February 1966), pp. 48–9
  First Love and Other Shorts (Grove Press, 1974)

Assez
> *Assez* (Les Éditions de Minuit, 1966)
> *La Quinzaine littéraire* 1 (15 March 1966), pp. 4–5

Enough
> *Books and Bookmen* 13 : 7 (April 1967), pp. 62–3
> *No's Knife: Collected Shorter Prose 1945–1966* (Calder, 1967)
> *First Love and Other Shorts* (Grove Press, 1974)

Le Dépeupleur
> *Le Dépeupleur* (Les Éditions de Minuit, 1970)

The Lost Ones
> *The Lost Ones* (Calder and Boyars, 1972)
> *The Lost Ones* (Grove Press, 1972)

Bing
> *Bing* (Les Éditions de Minuit, 1966)

Ping
> *Encounter* 28 : 2 (February 1967), pp. 25–6
> *Harper's Bazaar* 3067 (June 1967), pp. 120, 140
> *No's Knife: Collected Shorter Prose 1945–1966* (Calder, 1967)
> *First Love and Other Shorts* (Grove Press, 1974)

Sans
> *La Quinzaine littéraire* 82 (1 November 1969), pp. 3–4
> *Sans* (Les Éditions de Minuit, 1969)

Lessness
> *New Statesman* (1 May 1970), p. 635
> *Evergreen Review* 14.80 (July 1970), pp. 35–6
> *Lessness* (Signature Series: Signature 9) (Calder and Boyars, 1970)

Foirades
> 'Foirade I', *Minuit* 1 (November 1972), pp. 22–6

'Foirades II & III', *Minuit* 2 (January 1973), pp. 40–2
'Foirades IV & V', *Minuit* 4 (May 1973), pp. 71–2
Pour finir encore (Minuit, 1976)
Pour finir encore et autre foirades (Minuit, 1976)

Fizzles

'Still', with etchings by Stanley William Hayter (Milan: M'Arte Edizioni, 1974)
'Still', Signature Anthology: Signature 20 (Calder and Boyars, 1975)
'Still', *The Malahide Review* 33 (January 1975), pp. 9–10
'For to End Yet Again', *New Writing and Writers* 13 (John Calder Ltd, 1976 [1975]), pp. 9–14.
Foirades/Fizzles, with etchings by Jasper Johns, ed. Véra Lindsay (New York: Petersburg Press, 1976)
Fizzles (Grove Press, 1976)
For to End Yet Again and Other Fizzles (John Calder Ltd, 1976)
'Fizzle 1' ['He is barehead'], *Tri-Quarterly* (In the wake of the *Wake*) 38 (Winter 1977), pp. 163–7
'Sounds', *Essays in Criticism* 28 : 2 (April 1978), pp. 156–7
'Still 3', *Essays in Criticism* 28 : 2 (April 1978), pp. 156–7

As the Story Was Told

Günter Eich zum Gedächtnis, ed. Siegfried Unseld (Frankfurt a. Main: Suhrkamp, 1975), pp. 10–[13]
Chicago Review 33 : 2 (1982), pp. 76–7
As the Story Was Told: Uncollected and Late Prose (John Calder Ltd/Riverrun Press, 1990)

La Falaise

Celui qui ne peut se servir de mots: à Bram Van Velde (Montpellier: Fata Morgana, 1975).

The Cliff [translated by Edith Fournier]

The Complete Short Prose 1929–1989, ed. S. E. Gontarski (Grove Press, 1995) *neither*

Programme, première of 'neither', set to music by Morton Feldman, Rome, 12 June 1977

High Fidelity and Musical America (February 1979)

Journal of Beckett Studies 4 (Spring 1979), p. 5

Collections and Anthologies:

No's Knife: Collected Shorter Prose 1945–1966 (Calder and Boyars, 1967; repr. 1975) ['The Expelled', 'The Calmative' and 'The End', *Texts for Nothing*, 'From an Abandoned Work', 'Enough', 'Imagination Dead Imagine' and 'Ping']

Stories and Texts for Nothing (Grove Press, 1967)

Têtes-mortes (Les Éditions de Minuit, 1967) ['D'un ouvrage abandonné', 'Assez', 'Imagination morte imaginez', 'Bing'; 1972 reprint included 'Sans']

First Love and Other Shorts (Grove Press, 1974) ['First Love', 'From an Abandoned Work', 'Enough', 'Imagination Dead Imagine', 'Ping', 'Not I', 'Breath']

Six Residua (John Calder Ltd, 1978) ['From an Abandoned Work', 'Enough', 'Imagination Dead Imagine', 'Ping', 'Lessness' and 'The Lost Ones']

Rockaby and Other Short Pieces (Grove Press, 1981) ['Rockaby', 'Ohio Impromptu', 'All Strange Away', 'A Piece of Monologue']

Collected Shorter Prose 1945–1980 (John Calder Ltd, 1984)

The Complete Short Prose 1929–1989, ed. S. E. Gontarski (Grove Press, 1995)